1/7/10
25.95

D0928137

EVERYTHING
BUT A
CHRISTMAS EVE

EVERYTHING BUT A CHRISTMAS EVE

•

Holly Jacobs

AVALON BOOKS
NEW YORK

Published by Thomas Bouregy & Co., Inc.
160 Madison Avenue, New York, NY 10016

Library of Congress Cataloging-in-Publication Data

Jacobs, Holly, 1963–
    Everything but a Christmas Eve / Holly Jacobs.
        p. cm.
    ISBN 978-0-8034-9984-3 (hardcover)
    1. Single women—Fiction. 2. Grandmothers—Fiction. I. Title.
    PS3610.A35643E925 2009
    813'.6—dc22

                                                          2009025429
PRINTED IN THE UNITED STATES OF AMERICA
ON ACID-FREE PAPER
BY HADDON CRAFTSMEN, BLOOMSBURG, PENNSYLVANIA

This one is for all the Nana Vancy fans
who've written me (and her), for Erin,
who first fell in love with the Salos,
and Faith, who continued to
believe in them.

Prologue

"Silver Bells"

Vancy Bashalde Salo was bored, and the entire Salo family knew it. Which is why they'd all practically thrown her out of the house that day, insisting she go to lunch with her two oldest friends, affectionately known in the family as the "Silver Bells" because they were long since gray and were named Annabelle and Isabel.

Vancy hoped her friends would be more sympathetic than her family. She knew she was driving them all—from her husband, Bela, straight down to her grandchildren—crazy, but she couldn't seem to help herself. For years she'd fretted and worried about the Salo Family Wedding Curse. Whenever she'd thought about it, it had always been with capital letters, because cursing your own family to bad weddings . . . well, that

1

was the sort of thing that deserved capital letters, even if it had been an accidental curse.

She looked across the table at her oldest and dearest friends and told them about the curse, not for the first time. ". . . and so there I was, Vancy Bashalde, the prettiest girl in Erdely, Hungary—"

Isabel Henning interrupted and filled in, "And you planned the most elaborate, fancy wedding the town had ever seen."

Annabelle Conner picked up the thread. "But your Bela didn't show up, and you thought he'd deserted you, so you said something like, 'If I don't get my beautiful wedding, I hope he never gets one. Bela or any of his descendants,' or something to that effect." Annabelle paused. "I think that last part, tacking on his kids and such, was sort of mean-spirited, Vancy. I mean, you never met the kids he hadn't had yet, and *they* didn't leave you waiting at the altar."

"But Bela hadn't been there because he'd had an accident," Isabel supplied. "And when he showed up, you married him right away, without bothering with another fancy wedding. You'd learned that all you wanted was him."

Vancy realized she had probably mentioned the curse story once or twice . . . maybe more, but they were friends, so they should listen again. "And then when my children—"

This time Annabelle interrupted her. "—got married and had wedding disaster after wedding disaster, and none of them got their fancy nuptials, you remembered what you'd said, and because you're Hungarian—"

Isabel said, "—you knew words had meaning, and you realized that you'd cursed your own family. And you tried to break the curse with your grandchildren's weddings."

"But they didn't cooperate." Vancy spoke rapidly so her friends wouldn't interrupt and ruin her story. "First my namesake, Vancy, was stood up at the altar; then she met the love of her life and didn't wait for me to plan a wedding. Then my grandson, Noah, got dumped at his stag party and found out he was in love with an old friend, and he didn't let me plan the wedding."

"And then there was Dori, who didn't let you plan *her* wedding either," Isabel started.

Vancy broke in. "And Bill, my granddaughter Dori's new husband, figured it out. There'd never *been* a curse, because Bela and I broke it when we married without waiting to plan another wedding. That's the part you two forgot—the fact that I tried to soften the curse by adding that when someone in Bela's family cared more about the marriage than the wedding, the curse would be over. And Bela and I broke the curse ourselves."

"Yes, dear, we know." Isabel heaved a sigh, as if listening to the entire story again was a huge trial.

"You've told us this story a few times over the years." Annabelle patted her hand and shot a look at Isabel that Vancy didn't miss.

"And even if you hadn't," Annabelle continued, "that reporter boy who made your granddaughter Vancy's life miserable when he wrote that wedding-curse story gave the details. All the gory details. And Vancy, dear, there were a lot of gory details."

"So, Vancy, if you don't mind my saying—" Isabel started.

"Our saying," Annabelle corrected.

"Our saying. Annabelle and I don't understand this malaise. You should be celebrating the fact that, thanks in part to you, all three of your grandchildren are happily married, and the curse is broken. Your great-grandchildren . . . how many are there now?"

"Vancy and Matt have Chris and Ricky, and their little girl, who won't answer to anything but Fred."

"They named their daughter Fred?" Isabel sounded aghast, and Annabelle nodded her agreement.

"No, the boys were upset she was a girl and started *calling* her Fred . . . and it stuck. So, Fred she is. And both Dori and Callie are pregnant. They're both due any day now—two new babies before the end of the year. I swear they're racing to see who can get to the finish line first. They're giving Bill and Noah fits, because they're both such tomboys and won't let something like a little pregnancy slow them down."

"Vancy, it sounds like there's a lot going on to keep you busy . . . ," Annabelle said.

"Yes, I know, but I can't help it. I'm bored. I loved setting up the kids and planning their weddings. Even when the weddings all fell through, it was fun to plan. Now there's nothing. Rick and Chris are way too young for me to even think about matchmaking."

"So, why wait for them? There are plenty of single people in the world," Annabelle said. "Maybe you could help one of them—"

"Matchmake for someone else? Someone other than family?" Vancy rolled the idea around in her mind. She didn't see a downside to it. "I'm so very good at what I do, and there are so many single people in the world."

"It would be like shooting fish in a barrel," Annabelle chirruped gleefully. "You always say you have special abilities because you're Hungarian. So, pick someone at random. Someone single. I mean, you wouldn't want to use your skills on someone already married."

Vancy tried to think of someone single. Suddenly she remembered her Bela talking about someone just yesterday.

"Why, Bela just hired a new girl at the office. She's going to be more than a secretary, sort of an office manager. He said she was tall and blond, but I shouldn't be jealous, because he was rather fond of short and gray." She smiled at the thought. Her Bela was so sweet.

"And this girl, she tsked him during the interview and told him that he wouldn't know a pie chart from a spreadsheet even if one of them bit him in the butt."

"And he hired her anyway?" Isabel asked, once again aghast.

Vancy loved her friend, but Isabel spent a great portion of her life aghast at one thing or the other.

"He hired her *because* of it. Bela likes someone who isn't afraid of putting him in his place."

"Which explains why he married you," Isabel muttered.

Vancy heard her friend but ignored her. Her mind was too filled with matchmaking ideas, and she felt more excitement than she had in months and months. "Annabelle, you are a good friend. I think this may work."

"Oh, Annabelle, what have you done?" Isabel whispered.

Vancy ignored that as well. She was too excited about her new project.

There was no more Salo Family Wedding Curse, but there were plenty of single people in need of her help.

And she was going to start with Eve Allen, Salo Construction's new office manager.

Maybe by Christmas Eve, she'd have helped Eve find her soul mate.

No *maybe* about it.

When Vancy Bashalde Salo set her mind to something, she always achieved it.

Knowing that words had power, Vancy whispered as her friends were talking, "Eve Allen will be head over heels in love by Christmas Eve."

Chapter One

"It's Beginning to Look a Lot Like Christmas"

Eve Elisabeth Allen stood outside Salo Construction the Monday after Thanksgiving.

"I am confident. I am competent. I am going to rock this business."

She said the words, mantralike, wanting this job to be a success. Because she needed this job.

Her last job . . .

No, she wasn't going to think about her last job. She wasn't going to think about anything in her immediate past. She was simply going to concentrate on being the best office manager in the history of Salo Construction.

Mr. Salo had told her the office would be shutting down the week before Christmas through the week after New Year's. She was going to use that time to revamp their filing system and totally restructure their computer files.

She'd organize to her heart's content.

And truly, organizing was all she was going to allow her heart to be content with. When her pesky heart wanted more than creating order in the midst of chaos, she got into trouble. And Eve didn't need any more trouble.

She walked into the unassuming brick building and put her coat in the coat closet . . . which was stuffed with boxes that appeared to be filled with files.

She wasn't sure who'd been running the office, but she was sure they didn't have any idea how to do it.

"Good morning," an older woman who was walking out of Bela Salo's office called to her. Mr. Bela Salo was officially retired, and his grandson, Noah, was in charge of the company, but she wasn't sure Bela Salo knew that.

The woman coming from his office was tiny. Not even five feet tall, Eve would guess. And her hair was white—not gray—and fluffy. She smiled. "You must be Bela's new office manager."

Eve thrust a hand out. "Eve. Eve Allen. You must be Mrs. Salo?"

The woman took her hand and shook it as she nodded her head. "Vancy. Vancy Salo. Bela's wife."

"Nice to meet you, Mrs. Salo—"

"Now, Eve, I'm sure Bela told you we're not formal here. You just call me Nana Vancy. Everyone does."

Eve didn't know how to respond to that request. This was the boss' wife, and she couldn't call her Mrs. Salo once she'd specifically outlawed that, but she didn't feel comfortable calling her something as familiar as Nana Vancy.

Eve liked to keep a professional distance. It was a rule of sorts. She'd let it lapse just once, and look how that had ended.

"It's nice to meet you, ma'am."

"Well, I feel the same way. Sit with me for a minute, and tell me what you did before you came to work for us. I need to know you better."

Eve wasn't sure why Mrs. Salo needed to know her better, but she wasn't about to argue with the matriarch of the Salo family. "I worked at an advertising company as a personal assistant and decided that my skills weren't being fully realized there." Yes, Eve came to that conclusion when Pat, aka Pat the Rat, took her idea for a campaign and passed it off as his own.

It wasn't that Eve wanted a job in marketing; she knew where her strengths were—in organizing. But even so, she felt that the least Pat should have done was acknowledge that she'd given him his direction. That, and he shouldn't have cheated on her. Finding out he was cheating on her was the deal breaker. That he was cheating on her with her best friend, Naomi, only made it worse.

"And your favorite holiday?" Mrs. Salo asked in a

random sort of way. "Christmas, right? I mean, with a name like Eve, Christmas does come to mind."

Eve wanted to tell her, wrong. Absolutely not. The holiday that had once seemed so magical lost its glow when she was in kindergarten and Timmy Potter told her that there was no Santa Claus.

Still, Eve limped along, trying to rediscover her love of Christmas and ignoring that every holiday season her name became a source of joy for the kids at school. Christmas Eve. She sighed. She hated it.

And then in ninth grade, right before the winter holiday formal, she thought she'd rediscovered her Christmas joy. Timmy Potter, now Tim Potter and the star of the basketball team, asked her to the dance.

Yes, for the blink of an eye she'd thought that maybe she'd get over losing Santa and having her name become an annual source of torment.

Then Tim stood her up.

After that, well, Christmas seemed to be a season when things went wrong for her. Like the year her wisdom teeth got impacted, and she'd had them out and spent the holiday with a bruised face and ice bags. Or the year that she'd bought her parents a perfect, one-of-a-kind antique chair, only to have them announce they'd bought themselves the same, second-of-a-kind chair. They said they were thrilled to have a set, but truly, somehow, every year Christmas lost a little more of its sparkle.

This holiday looked to be a bit depressing. After her Pat the Rat incident two weeks ago, she hadn't been looking forward to pretending to enjoy any family festivities. But it turned out that her parents were heading to the Bahamas, where they'd rented a house for a month, and they had promised they'd all celebrate in January. Eve took that as a sign that the universe had agreed she should take the holiday off.

This year she was going to ignore Christmas. She wasn't planning to fa-la-la or deck any halls. No cookies and milk left out on Christmas Eve and no frantic holiday shopping.

No, she'd simply come into the quiet Salo office and work while everyone else went Christmas crazy. With luck, by January she'd be over her breakup pain and ready to celebrate the holiday with her parents.

But she didn't say anything about any of this to her boss' wife. She simply shook her head and wondered how long it would be until the woman left. "No, Christmas really isn't my favorite holiday."

"New Year's Eve?" Mrs. Salo pressed.

Eve had no particular affection for New Year's Eve, but this woman was obviously not going to stop until she had an answer, so Eve nodded. "Yes. Love New Year's Eve. It's . . . uh . . . a time of new beginnings. What's not to love?"

That was it! This year—well, technically next year—she'd celebrate starting anew on New Year's. In December she'd mourn her ex, settle into her new job, ignore Christmas, and by January first she'd be ready to start fresh.

"And your favorite color?" Mrs. Salo continued.

Eve couldn't imagine why the woman needed to know her favorite color.

To the best of her knowledge, she didn't have one. She liked colors but not one more than any other. But she shrugged and said, "Red," because it was the first color to come to mind after their Christmas discussion.

"And kids? Do you like kids?"

Eve nodded. She did like kids. From a distance.

Up close they tended to be whiny, sticky, or simply smelly.

"And if you had a genie's lamp and could have one wish, what would it be?"

Eve wondered if Mrs. Salo had something wrong with her . . . mentally. She couldn't think of a gentle way to ask and didn't want to agitate her if she did, so she simply said, "I'd go to Ireland."

"Oh, are you Irish?"

"No. English and German. But still, it just looks so green. Hey, maybe green's my favorite color."

"Well, then, green it is." Mrs. Salo seemed delighted with Eve's sudden certainty about a favorite color.

"Oh, one last, very important question: Do you have a boyfriend?"

"No, ma'am. No boyfriend. And no real desire for one." That was the biggest understatement ever.

"Of course, you'll feel differently when the right

man comes along." Mrs. Salo stood. "It's been lovely talking with you. I really wanted to get to know a bit about you. Salo Construction is a family business. So, if you're working here, you're part of the family. Have you met everyone yet?"

"I've met your husband and grandson, Noah. My understanding is that your granddaughter Dori spends most of her time on location and that your other granddaughter, Vancy, is a lawyer who, although she work for Salo's, doesn't have an office here but occasionally uses the conference room."

"That's right, but they'll be in here a lot, despite all that."

"Well, I look forward to meeting them."

What Eve really looked forward to was Mrs. Salo's leaving so she could start organizing the office. There was something so comforting about putting things into order. She glanced around the room and knew there was certainly a lot of order needed. And she could use all the comfort that would create.

"Well, I think meeting everyone is going to happen sooner than you intended," Mrs. Salo said happily. "You see, I wanted to invite you to our house for dinner tonight. A sort of welcome to the family."

"Pardon?"

"As I said, Salo Construction is family owned and family run, so if you're working here, then you're part of the family."

"But—"

"Now, I'll see you at the house right after work. You just follow Noah over."

"But—"

"And welcome to Salo's, Eve. I think you're really going to like working here."

Eve watched as Mrs. Salo breezed out of the office. She sank into her chair, laid her head back, and stared at the ceiling. "What on earth was that?"

"Was what?" Noah Salo asked. He had dark hair that looked as if it should be combed. But despite his less than tidy appearance, he seemed like a nice enough man.

Eve sat back up. "Mr. Salo, I'm sorry. I just met your grandmother, and I—"

" 'Nuf said," he assured her with a grin. "Nana has always been . . . interesting, but ever since my youngest sister got married and that left her no one's wedding to meddle with, she's been more of a handful than ever."

"You and your siblings are all married?"

"Happily so. My wife and sister are both expecting around Christmas."

"Well, congratulations. It looks as if I'll be meeting them tonight. Your grandmother . . ." Insisted. Decreed. ". . . *asked* me to dinner."

"I know my grandmother, Eve. *Asking* is a very kind way of phrasing her dinner invitation. I just hope it doesn't interfere with your plans." He looked contrite.

Though Eve had hoped to order in dinner at the office and work on the horribly disorganized filing system, she found herself smiling and saying, "It was very sweet of her."

Noah snorted. "I hope you think that after you've attended a Salo family meal. I'm not sure how she's going to manage getting everyone together on a Monday night, especially since we all just ate together on Thanksgiving."

"Oh, maybe she'll need to reschedule?" Eve made the sentence a question, hoping that's what would happen.

Noah shook his head. "Don't get your hopes up. If Nana's declared that everyone's coming to dinner, then everyone will be there. Just remember, I'll be there too, for moral support."

And on that ominous note, Noah Salo walked back to his office.

Eve watched him leave and wondered just what she'd gotten herself into.

TC Potter opened the garment bag and stared at the red coat and pants.

"Not exactly a fashion statement, is it, Bert?"

His English bulldog, Bert, snuffled in what TC took as sympathy, though it was hard to tell—Bert always snuffled. It had something to do with his rather smooshed-in bulldog nose. The smooshed-in face also led to Bert's being the worst snorer ever. The fact that the dog insisted on sleeping near TC meant he'd spent a number of sleepless nights at first, but eventually he'd learned to sleep through the dog's thunderous slumber.

"What do you think?" He reached into a pocket of the bag and slipped a white beard and wig into place.

Bert instantly started barking and looking around the house for TC.

"You are not the brightest dog in the world," TC said affectionately, and he pulled off the wig. He was about to remove the beard when the doorbell rang.

His heart sank.

For the last year, answering the door had become an iffy proposition. The only thing worse was getting the mail.

With his luck, it would be a postal worker with another of those plastic boxes telling him that there were too many letters to fit in his mailbox.

TC crept to the front door and peeked out the small peephole. Nothing.

The doorbell rang again, but still he saw nothing.

Maybe it was a kid selling candy bars. That wouldn't be too bad. TC had no inherent problems with kids. And though he was no chocolate addict, he didn't mind it.

He opened the door.

Mrs. Salo from next door stood poised to ring the bell again. She smiled when she saw him. "Hello, TC."

Mrs. Salo wasn't a chocolate-selling kid, but she was a nice surprise.

"Come on in," he said as he opened the door wider.

The Salos were perfect neighbors. Other than inviting

him to an occasional family meal, they were quiet and left him alone for the most part. Occasionally the twins would come over and sell him something, but that was about it.

Neighbors who only required a hello or good-bye wave and the purchase of an occasional school candy bar were perfect in his book.

"I love the beard, TC," Mrs. Salo teased.

She must have reminded Bert, because on cue, the dog started barking again.

"Sorry." He pulled it off, and the placated Bert wandered into the living room and flopped in front of the fireplace. "Did you need something?"

Mrs. Salo didn't answer his question. Instead she asked, "The beard?"

"Oh, if you promise not to tell, I'll explain. I'm doing another article for my Every American Man series. Next week's job is a mall Santa."

"Oh, that's a lovely job. Does that mean you like Christmas? And what about New Year's Eve?"

He shrugged. "They're all right."

"Your middle name?"

He had no idea why she was asking, but he said, "Christopher. Timothy Christopher."

"Ah, TC. I see. And your favorite color?"

TC wasn't sure that he had a favorite color, and he especially wasn't sure why his neighbor would ask, but he liked Mrs. Salo. Oh, she was a bit different, but different in a good way. He'd kept the reporters off his property when they'd wanted to use it to take pictures of the Salos during the height of their Family Wedding Curse tabloid fiasco, and they'd returned the favor by keeping women off their property when the more serious ones sought an audience with one of America's Most Eligible Bachelors. So he answered the first color that came to mind. "Green."

Mrs. Salo grinned. "Yes, you'll do nicely."

"For what?" he asked, totally confused.

"Dinner. Come over to the house at six for dinner tonight."

It wasn't a request, it was a decree. And he wasn't sure how having green as a favorite color got him a dinner. "Mrs. Salo—"

"Nana Vancy—or just Nana, if you prefer—remember? We're close, TC. More than just neighbors."

That was the first he'd heard of their closeness. As a matter of fact, their lack of closeness had been one of the wonderful things about having the Salos as neighbors.

Waving, candy bars, and reciprocal repelling of pests.

Not wanting to foster this new supposed closeness, he said, "Really, I couldn't—"

"Nonsense. I'll see you at six. And you're welcome to bring Bert. The boys will love to play with him."

And before he could come up with any excuse, Mrs. Salo—Nana Vancy—walked out the door.

What on earth was that all about?

"Well, Bert, I don't see any way around it. Looks like you and I are going to dinner at the Salos tonight."

Bert barked, and TC wasn't sure if it was a bark of happiness or dread.

TC was leaning toward dread himself.

After all, when a woman—no matter what her age—changed her habits, it didn't bode well.

So, Mrs. Salo's moving from a wave-on-occasion neighbor to a Nana-Vancy, meal-providing one was ominous.

TC glanced at the clock.

Four hours from now he'd know what was going on.

Chapter Two

"Do You Hear What I Hear?"

Eve didn't follow Noah to the Salos after all. Instead, Noah followed her to her house and then drove her because he said his grandmother's street became a parking nightmare when the entire Salo clan converged. And anytime anyone in the family could carpool, they did.

Eve wanted to point out that she wasn't in the family but decided that contradicting her new boss probably wasn't in her best interest, so she'd agreed.

She wasn't sure what she'd expected, but the chaos that greeted her as she walked into the small house wasn't it. It wasn't just the lines of boots that were scattered in the entryway or the piles of coats that were slung over the railing because the closet was open and obviously filled beyond its capacity. . . . It was the noise.

The dull roar of a crowd.

"Just throw your stuff anywhere," Noah said as he tossed his own coat onto the teetering pile.

Eve took her boots off and placed them neatly in a vacant space, then put her coat on top of the others after stuffing her hat, gloves, and scarf into a sleeve.

"Okay, the best thing to do is take a deep breath and just dive in," Noah said, in what she was sure was meant to be a helpful and encouraging suggestion but in the end just led to a terrifying sense of what-had-she-gotten-herself-into.

She followed him into a small living room that was filled with people. "Everyone," Noah called, "this is our new office manager, Eve Allen. Eve, this is . . ."

He pointed and rattled off names, walking as he went farther into the house, still pointing and naming.

She was sure she would never match a name to a face. The names all jumbled together. Callie, Vancy—but this one wasn't Mrs. Call-Me-Nana-Vancy Salo but a younger woman—Dori, Bill, Matt, Chris and Rick—twin boys she'd never tell apart—a toddling little girl everyone called Fred . . . After the little girl, Eve just gave up and nodded.

"I think that's everyone," Noah said, their tour having ended in the kitchen. "I think they've all met her, Nana."

"Good. Now, Eve, *kedvenc,* why don't you have a seat at the counter, and we'll visit as I put the finishing touches on my cabbage rolls? Noah, would you send TC back?"

Noah looked confused, but that didn't come as any shock to Eve. This house seemed primed to cause confusion. And though Mrs. Salo was one of its tinier members, Eve was pretty sure that Nana Vancy was at the center of most of the confusion.

Noah was obviously accustomed to not knowing what was going on, because he simply smiled and said, "Sure, Nana."

The moment he'd jumped back into the throng, Nana said, "Now, Eve, dear, tell me—"

Whatever Mrs. Salo wanted her to tell was lost in bloodcurdling screams coming from one of the other rooms.

A tall man with brown hair strode into the kitchen. "Fred was happy to see Bert when we arrived."

"That was a scream of happiness?" Eve asked.

The man noticed her for the first time. "Yes. I'm pretty sure it was." The man stopped and studied her. "Hi. You're a Salo I haven't met yet. I'm TC, the Salos' neighbor."

"I'm not a Salo, just an employee. Eve."

"There's no 'just' about it, Eve," Nana Vancy scolded. "You're a valued part of Salo Construction."

"I just started today, ma'am. I haven't had time to be valued yet, but I plan to be."

TC grinned. "Congratulations on the new job, Eve. Now, Nana Vancy, you needed something?"

"I need a man with a strong arm to mash the potatoes." She pulled out an old-fashioned potato ricer. "I know that a lot of people like to use a mixer, but that makes the potatoes too smooth. This is the best method. Sometimes the old ways are the best ways."

Mrs. Salo produced a huge pot of potatoes, tossed a stick of butter into them, and sloshed a bunch of milk in as well.

"Now, mash," she instructed.

Eve didn't ask why Mrs. Salo hadn't simply had Noah mash the potatoes. She'd already come to the conclusion that asking why about Mrs. Salo was like asking why about the weather. With either force of nature, there was no rhyme or reason; there was just the way things were.

"Now, Eve, TC here is quite a star. Last year, *Famous Magazine* named him one of the country's most eligible bachelors. Isn't that lovely?"

"Congratulations," she said, because frankly she didn't have any idea what else to say about news like that.

TC rammed the potato masher up and down in the pot and started to look a bit flushed.

"Nothing to get excited about. I'd written a few articles, and the editor read them and—" He stopped mashing a moment and shook his head. "Well, the rest just happened."

"After he was named a most eligible bachelor, TC wrote one of his columns about the experience of being named an eligible bachelor and being photographed and such. 'My Month as a Male Model,'" Nana said helpfully. She was doing something to the contents of an industrial-sized pan. "Women all over the country wanted him."

"Well, I've been told that having a lot of women want you is every man's dream, so congratulations again." The words came out more tinged with bitterness than Eve had intended. Pat the Rat had certainly wanted more than his fair share of women.

"And TC loves the color green. It's his favorite," Mrs. Salo said. "It's Eve's, too."

Eve didn't like the particular gleam in Mrs. Salo's eyes as she made her favorite-color pronouncement, so she quickly said, "Actually, I decided it was red. Yes, red is definitely my favorite color."

Nana turned and looked disappointed. "Well, TC's going to be playing Santa Claus at the mall."

"Just for the week. It's going to be the basis for my next column. I'd hoped for a little more out-of-the-way Santa job, but when you sign the contract with Holiday, Inc., you agree to go where sent, so the mall it is."

"Have fun." Eve was pretty sure that playing a Santa at the mall would be her idea of torture.

"Maybe I should go mingle, Mrs. Salo." Eve knew she should offer to help with the meal and join in the conversation Mrs. Salo wanted, but she sensed there was more than potato mashing afoot and decided retreat was the better part of valor.

Before either Mrs. Salo or her eligible bachelor could say anything else, Eve slipped into the very crowded dining room.

She'd originally hoped to just come to dinner and make her break as quickly as possible.

Her new goal was to avoid the playing-Santa, potato-mashing, most-eligible-bachelor for the evening, because unless she was very much mistaken, he was the reason she'd been invited to dinner.

TC had moved in next door to the Salos two years earlier, and he'd been invited to an occasional meal in the past and always enjoyed the Salo family's company.

But tonight it was uncomfortable.

Everyone kept shooting Nana Vancy strange looks, and she would square her shoulders and stare them all down. Then she'd start some inane conversational ploy between him and Eve Allen.

He now knew that Eve liked the color red, that her favorite flowers were daisies, that she liked New Year's Eve better than Christmas Eve, and that her favorite food was oatmeal.

He looked up at that answer, thinking that oatmeal sounded like a very bland choice, and he caught the quickest whisper of a smile on Eve's face and realized she'd been kidding.

Nana Vancy didn't realize that, and neither, apparently, did the rest of the family, as they all stared at her, but Eve had ignored the looks and simply gone on eating her cabbage roll and answering Nana Vancy's strange questions.

By dessert TC realized what was going on, and immediately after he did, he realized Eve had figured it out before she'd answered "oatmeal."

Nana Vancy was trying to fix the two of them up.

He had no idea why.

He'd never done anything to suggest he was looking to be fixed up. As a matter of fact, he was pretty sure he'd done just about everything he could to indicate that he didn't want to be fixed up. Hiding from women seeking a Most Eligible Bachelor should have given his neighbor a hint.

He finished Nana Vancy's delicious chocolate cake, then started hemming and hawing about needing to get back home because tomorrow was his first day at his new job.

"Well, we're sorry to see you go. I'm sure Eve needs to get home as well, since tomorrow is her second day at her new job. Would you mind driving her home for me?"

TC hadn't come up with a suitable excuse because he hadn't seen that particular request coming, which was why, ten minutes later, after slowly making their way past the many members of the Salo family and putting on coats and boots and sludging across the snow-covered grass that separated the Salos' and his drive, he'd loaded Bert and his unwanted passenger into his truck.

"Where to?" he asked.

Eve gave him her address—an upper eastside address—then added, "Sorry about that."

"About what?"

"Don't play stupid. There's no way anyone could miss that Mrs. Salo was trying to fix us up. But I honestly don't have a clue why. She just met me today."

"I've lived next door to the Salos for two years, and nothing like this has ever happened before."

"Well, I just didn't want you to think I instigated that. . . ." She paused as if she were unsure what to call the setup. *Debacle* came to mind. *Farce* was a close second. Both might insult TC, so she didn't finish the sentence.

"Same here. I have no interest in dating. If I did, there are still letters trickling in from last year's column. I could pick any one of those women to date."

"Well, then, that's settled. We can relax." She reached between them and patted Bert's head, which put the dog into a rapturous high. Sure he'd found a new friend, he plopped his head into Eve's lap.

"Oh, you might want to make him move. He drools when he sleeps."

She laughed and stroked the dog's ears. "I'm not worried about a little dog drool."

That was not the usual response. In TC's experience, women were not only not fond of dog drool, they were repulsed by it.

He turned and glanced at the woman riding with

him. She was tall. He liked that. At six one, he tended to tower over women, and he didn't enjoy that. He liked a woman who came close to looking him in the eye. Eve had nice, blondish brown hair and blue eyes. She looked girly enough to hate dog drool.

He realized that with all the inane things he now knew about her, he didn't know much of the usual information. "So, Nana Vancy said you're from Erie? Where'd you go to school?"

"Well, actually, in Greene Township, just barely outside Erie."

"Eve . . ." He glanced at her, a memory slowly taking shape. "Eve . . . What's your last name?"

"Allen."

It was one of those lightbulb moments. TC hadn't sensed anything familiar about Eve, but he definitely remembered the name *Eve Allen*. "I remember you. TC Potter. Tim, back then."

After a brief pause he heard, "And it was Timmy before that, right?" There was no happy-to-see-you-again tone to her comment. In fact, the word *Timmy* came out sort of snarl-like.

"Yes," he admitted slowly and cautiously. "Timmy. Back in grade school."

"Yes, I know. Timmy Potter. The boy who felt he needed to tell the entire kindergarten class there was no such thing as Santa Claus."

TC concentrated on the road; he didn't need to glance across the car to know that Eve didn't recall the incident fondly. "I don't remember doing it, but Mom loves to tell the story about when the teacher called her to say I'd made the entire kindergarten cry. It might be a little late, but, sorry."

"That one is easy to forgive. I mean, if not you, one of the older kids was bound to tell us. But standing me up our freshman year for the winter holiday formal? That's a little harder to forgive. Of course, you didn't make the entire kindergarten cry over that one—" She snapped her mouth shut, cutting off her own sentence.

But TC knew what she'd been about to say. He hadn't made the entire kindergarten class cry over that one, just her.

He also remembered with vivid clarity why he'd canceled their date. "I guess I need to say I'm sorry for that one too" was all he offered her.

"No, it's fine. You helped me grow up—both times—TC." That was the last word she said before the truck pulled up in front of her house, and she said, "Thank you for the lift."

She gently lifted Bert's head with one hand and started to open her door with the other.

"Hey, maybe you'd let me take you out to dinner sometime and make both the Santa exposé and the dance up to you."

She frowned. "No, I'm sure that's not necessary."

"But I'd really like to."

Eve had managed to get out of the truck without

waking Bert, and she said, "But I really wouldn't. Thank you again for the ride."

She shut the door quietly, so as not to wake the dog.

There was nothing left to do but back out of the driveway of her cute little brick home and head back to his house.

He couldn't believe he'd asked Eve Allen out.

He should have been relieved that she'd said no. But for some reason he didn't understand, *relieved* was not the word he'd use to describe what he was feeling.

TC searched for the proper word.

Disappointed.

He was disappointed.

What on earth was with that?

The next day, Eve was sitting in a corner of the office surrounded by stacks of files. Piles and piles of files.

She hummed as she worked. The new system was going to be great. When she was done, she'd be able to find any given file in seconds. And with her instruction, so could the rest of the Salo Construction team.

"Eve, I'm so glad I found you," Mrs. Salo said as she entered the office, a whirlwindish feeling about her.

That was just it. Mrs. Salo produced a feeling in Eve of being blown about with no control.

As if to punctuate the observation, a cloud of snow flew in just before Nana shut the door.

Eve ignored the sinking sensation in the pit of her stomach and forced a smile. "I'm so glad to see you, ma'am. I wanted to thank you again for the dinner last night."

"Oh, it was my pleasure. I always cook too much food."

Eve picked up the nearest file and held up it in Mrs. Salo's direction, hoping she'd get the hint that Eve was busy. "Well, I'd better get back to work before your grandson fires me."

"Well, I stopped in because I hoped that Noah could do a favor for me. I'm going back to see him." Mrs. Salo didn't wait for Eve to respond; she just hurried down the hall.

Eve hadn't heard the door, and only a minute could have passed when Mrs. Salo came back into the reception area. "Noah said he can't help me. But he did say I could ask you. You'd be doing it on company time."

"Sure, Mrs. Salo." Eve set the file down and stood. "What can I do for you?"

"I need you to drive to the mall at four-thirty and give TC a ride home."

"Pardon?" Trapped. She was trapped. "I'm not sure—"

"TC called this morning. All four of the tires on his truck were flat when he went to leave for work. I drove him to the mall and promised to pick him up at four-thirty, but I forgot I have a doctor's appointment, and at my age . . ." Mrs. Salo paused and gave a dramatic cough. "At my age I can't afford to miss one. So I'm hoping you'll pick him up."

Eve had a horrible mental image of Mrs. Salo tiptoeing through the snow between her house and TC's, creeping into his garage, and deflating all four tires.

Yet as she looked at the diminutive older lady, she knew that was absurd.

Eve was just a bit too paranoid, that was all.

And though the last thing she wanted to do was pick up the man who was once the boy who'd stood her up, she couldn't see any way out of it. "Sure. I'll get him for you and see him home."

"Oh, Eve, you are a treasure, *kedvenc.* Now I've got to run. Don't forget, four-thirty. Actually, you probably should get there a few minutes early, since he'll be expecting me and won't know to look for you. He's in front of Wagner's Department Store, right up the hall from Borders bookstore."

"I know where it is, ma'am."

"Nana Vancy," Mrs. Salo corrected. "Everyone calls me that. Even TC. You can do it, Eve. Come on. Nana Vancy."

"Nana Vancy," Eve parroted on cue.

"That didn't hurt, now, did it?" the older woman teased. "Now, you won't forget TC? You probably should leave in an hour."

"I won't forget," she promised.

"Thank you. Now, you come over again soon for another dinner, all right?"

"Yes, ma'am." Mrs. Salo just looked at her. It was the same sort of look her mom gave her, and Eve corrected herself. "Nana Vancy."

"You're a good girl, Eve. I knew that the minute I met you. No, I knew that the minute Bela told me about your interview. He was quite taken with you, my Bela. Though he said there was a bit of a loneliness about you."

"No, Nana Vancy, there's no loneliness about me at all. I've got a very busy and people-filled life. Why, sometimes there are so many people milling about, clamoring for dates and outings, that I long for a little lonely."

It was a good and valiant try, Eve told herself, but Nana's expression said she wasn't buying it. "Well, you can't have too many friends, *kedvenc*. And speaking of friends, don't forget TC."

"I won't . . . Nana."

"Good girl."

There was no hope of forgetting TC Potter. After all these years, she'd never forgotten Timmy or Tim Potter. She was sure she'd never forget his newest incarnation, TC, either. He was the sort of man who stuck out in a woman's memory. And, due to her particular circumstances, she'd thought of him every Christmas since kindergarten.

But just because she thought of him didn't mean she wanted to date him.

Even if she hadn't been able to convince Nana

Vancy of that fact, she'd pretty much spelled it out to TC last night. He wouldn't misinterpret her picking him up.

And just in case he did, she'd be clear again: TC Potter was the last man she'd ever want to date.

TC lifted yet another child into his lap. He'd started counting when he began his shift, but somewhere around thirty he'd lost track. All he knew was, he'd held a lot of kids in his lap today.

Tiny infants who made him nervous due to a gut-twisting fear that he'd drop them, to slightly soggy or sticky toddlers, to kids too old for Santa's lap—he'd held them all, posed for pictures, and listened to wish lists from those who were old enough to articulate objects of desire.

He tried to come up with lines for his Every American Man series as he lifted a particularly husky six-year-old off his lap and handed him to his mom. The woman didn't look strong enough to hold the boy, and, frankly, the kid was far too old to be held.

Santa's sciatica silently screamed. . . . Not that he had problems with sciatica, but if he had to do this job for more than a week, he might. *Santa turns Scrooge. . . .*

Now, that was a possibility.

Seriously, if one more kid put a finger in his or her nose while they sat on his lap, he was going to quit.

He looked up to see if he had another Christmas

wisher to hold, and he saw Eve Allen standing outside the white fence that surrounded Santa's Village.

He got up off his chair, thankful for an excuse to stretch his legs, and walked over to her. "Ho, ho, ho, little girl. Have you been good this year?"

"The fact that I'm here, offering you a ride home, would make me fairly confident answering yes to that question."

"What happened to Nana Vancy? She offered to pick me up."

Eve just stood there, staring at him, a look of expectancy on her face.

And finally it hit him. "Oh. She set this up."

Eve nodded.

"You really don't think a woman Nana Vancy's age crept over to my house, got into my garage, and let the air out of all my tires, do you?"

"Do you?" she countered.

It sounded absurd when he said it, but as he thought about it, TC could indeed imagine his neighbor doing just that.

"Yes. Yes, I do."

"I thought it was absurd at first, but the more I've considered it, the more I believe she did. So let's just be clear: This isn't a date, and I had nothing to do with it."

"We're clear all right."

"I just wanted to let you know I was here. I'm heading down to the bookstore and will wait for you there."

"I'll be done in about ten minutes."

"See you then."

Eve flounced down the mall, and TC went back to Santa's chair to take care of the four kids in line.

But as he listened to Christmas wishes, he kept thinking about his elderly neighbor letting the air out of his tires in order to force him to spend time with Eve.

And, rather than being annoyed, for some reason he felt grateful.

He liked Eve Allen.

Of course, she'd made it clear that she wasn't interested in anything even remotely date-ish with him.

Maybe that was part of the attraction. After a year of women chasing him, it felt nice to have one who wasn't the least bit impressed that he was one of America's Most Eligible Bachelors.

He wasn't looking to change that status, but the idea of a few dates with Eve was very appealing.

At least to him.

He suspected that dating him wasn't the least bit appealing to Eve.

And for some reason he couldn't fathom, he really wanted to change her mind.

He planned to start as soon as he got out of his Santa outfit.

Fifteen minutes later, a vague plan for dinner on his mind, he found Eve in the back of the bookstore with a pile of paperbacks in hand.

"I seem to remember your reading a lot in high

school, so I guess it shouldn't surprise me to see you with an armful of books," he teased.

Eve frowned when he mentioned high school, and TC could have kicked himself. Reminding Eve that he'd stood her up was not the tactic he should employ to win her over. "Just take your time and finish shopping," he said.

"I'm done." Her tone was flat and slightly annoyed. "Just give me a minute to check out."

She paid and was ready to go in short order.

"Here, let me take the bag for you," he offered.

"I was capable of carrying my books in school, and I still am now."

Great, Potter, he scolded himself. He was making a total muck of this. He tried again. "I was hoping you'd let me buy you dinner as a thank-you. This was a huge favor."

"No, that's not necessary. I'm here on the company's time, so it's not as if I'm really doing you a favor. I'm being paid for it."

Ouch. That sort of hurt. "But I'd really like to take you to dinner. I haven't been to the new restaurant in the Boston Store yet, have you?"

"No."

The Boston Store was one of Erie's landmarks. Generations of people had shopped there, frequently meeting up with companions under the department store's huge clock. The phrase "Meet me under the clock" was common back in the day, which is what had given the new restaurant its name. "Under the Clock is supposed to be great. The plates even look like clocks. Come on. It's beautiful. You have to eat. I have to eat. . . ."

Eve sighed. "Fine. As long as we're perfectly clear that this is not a date. We'll go dutch."

"Deal."

"And let's also be clear that I'm saying yes not because I have some overwhelming need to spend time with you. It's just because I'd have to go home and fix something, and this seems easier."

"Got it. It's a convenient dinner, not a date, and you're paying your own way."

She nodded and looked relieved. "Yes." She paused and suddenly added, "Oh, and one more stipulation."

"Name it."

"Do not ever, even under pain of torture, tell Nana Vancy about this."

He grinned. "My lips are sealed."

"Good, because goodness knows what she'd do if she thought her plan was working."

"Yes, goodness knows." TC tried to make it sound as if the idea of Nana Vancy's plan working was as off-putting to him as it obviously was to Eve, but he wasn't quite sure he managed it.

Eve frowned in his direction but didn't say anything else.

They had a delightful meal. Maybe it was the fact that she'd clarified their non-date status, but Eve seemed to relax. They talked books, and it turned out they were both Frank Herbert fans and had been following the new Dune books his son was writing.

They talked about downtown Erie's revitalization, the Boston Store's being a great example of how the downtown was coming back to life.

They talked and ate, and TC couldn't remember the last time he'd enjoyed himself with a woman so much. He was sure it was before he'd become a Most Eligible Bachelor.

It was almost seven when Eve pulled into his driveway.

"Now, remember, don't say a word about this to your neighbor," she warned him.

"I won't," he assured her. Something bright pink caught his eye, and he laughed. "But I don't think it will do any good."

"Why?" Eve asked.

"Because here she comes."

Eve didn't even try to stifle her groan.

TC started humming the theme song of *Jaws,* which made Eve frown.

Moments later Nana Vancy was knocking on the passenger window. TC rolled it down. "Hi, Nana."

"TC, I'm glad you're home. Matt came over this afternoon to pick up the boys, and before he left, he and Bela came over and filled your tires. They didn't see any leaks but said you should check to see that they're all holding air."

"I will, Nana." A thought occurred to him. "How

did they get into my garage? After the trouble last night, I double-checked that it was locked before we left this morning."

"You gave me the code, remember?"

He didn't remember. As a matter of fact, he was pretty sure he hadn't. But looking at Nana's diminutive stature and sweet smile, he doubted himself and simply said, "Well, thank you so much, and please tell Bela and Matt thanks too."

"We're your neighbors. That's what neighbors do."

"How was your doctor's appointment?" Eve asked.

Nana Vancy looked confused. "My what?"

"Your appointment. The one you had to go to instead of picking up TC."

The elderly woman's face cleared. "Oh, that. It's fine. The doctor said I was as healthy as a horse."

"I'm glad," Eve said, but she shot TC a look that said, *You see? It was a setup.*

"And you two? Did you go out after TC finished work?"

TC was about to say yes, when Eve said, "No. TC had to work late, so I waited at the mall and did some shopping. See the bags on the backseat?" She pointed.

Nana looked disappointed. "So, no date?"

"No. But I'm ahead on my Christmas shopping, so it was all good," Eve said, chipper and festive. "Well, good night, TC."

It was a not-so-subtle hint. TC took it and got out. "Thanks again for *everything*." He put emphasis on the last word, hoping she realized he was thanking her for the dinner as well as the ride.

"You're welcome."

She backed away, leaving him with Nana Vancy in his snow-covered drive.

"So, TC, you're playing Santa Claus for the rest of the week?"

"Yes. Holiday, Inc., signed me up to play Santa there for a week, just as I requested."

"Holiday, Inc.?"

"They're a temp agency geared specifically toward the holidays. It's a crapshoot where they send you. But they understood that this was for an article, and they helped me out, even though I had to sign the standard contract, just for liability's sake."

"A holiday temp agency with a contract. Now, isn't that a smart idea? Holiday, Inc. I'll remember that." There was a hint of something TC couldn't quite identify in Nana Vancy's tone.

Something he wasn't sure he wanted to identify, because he suspected she might be up to another flat-tire trick to throw him together with Eve . . . and, he discovered, he really didn't mind at all.

"I need your help." Vancy Bashalde Salo looked at her husband and grandson, Noah, the next morning.

"Nana, whatever you . . ." Noah paused and looked at her, then changed his statement of unconditional support to a question. "What do you need?"

She passed him a Post-it with a phone number on it. "This is Holiday, Inc. I need you to call them and hire TC's Santa services next week."

Noah took the note and studied it, while Bela asked, "Why does Salo Construction need TC's services?"

"Because he's going to deliver Salo Construction's employees and subcontractors our holiday bonuses and gifts. And . . ." She reached into her purse and pulled out a list. "He's also going to deliver Salo Construction's gifts to the children in hospitals in Erie. We've decided that we've been so blessed that we should give more back to the community, and children in the hospital are a great place to give back. These are the names of the charge nurses on their floors."

Noah looked at the list, then handed it to Bela. "Where did these names come from, Nana?"

"I called the hospitals. It didn't take long."

"And we're going to hire TC to play Santa Claus for us?"

"Yes. Of course, with all our employees, subcontractors, and the kids, he'll probably need some help with both the shopping and delivering. Did I say he'd be purchasing most of the gifts too?"

"And who do you suggest assist our Santa?" Noah asked.

"Why, Eve, of course. She's our office manager, someone who's here to help pick up the overflow. This is overflow."

"Nana, would this have anything to do with the

impromptu family dinner the other night? The family dinner that included both TC—a nice neighbor who until Monday didn't make a habit out of joining us at family meals—and Eve, a new employee?"

The jig was up. Vancy could see that both Bela and Noah knew exactly what she was doing. That was okay with Vancy. She could use it to her advantage.

More specifically, she could use her husband to her advantage. "Now, Bela," she said, bypassing her grandson, "you know how bored I've been since the curse was lifted. Relieved but bored. Isabel and Annabelle suggested—"

"Oh, not the Silver Bells." Noah groaned. "Papa, you can't aid Nana in anything the Bells suggested."

"Noah, I will not have you talk about my oldest and dearest friends so disrespectfully," she scolded.

"I'm sorry, Nana." He didn't sound all that sorry.

"You're forgiven. But, Bela, they suggested that maybe I should try my hand at matchmaking. I can't explain why I chose Eve and TC, other than to say that they feel right for each other. And you know that with my Hungarian background, I'm extrasensitive. I'm not going to force anything, but, Bela, if they work together on this little project, they may find my feeling was correct."

"And if they don't?" Noah asked.

"I'll think of something else."

Bela shook his head. "No, you'll stop meddling."

"Fine. If you set up my Santa project, and at the end of it they're not in love, I'll stop." She crossed her fingers as she said the words.

"Done," Bela said.

"But, Papa," Noah protested, "you're retired, and I'm in charge of Salo Construction, and I don't think—"

"It would be wise to show our appreciation to our employees or the people we work with?" Bela asked.

"Well, no. That's a good idea, but—"

"You don't think we should accept some social obligations after how lucky this family has been, especially considering how horrible it would be to be a child in the hospital at Christmastime? What if it were Chris, Ricky, or Fred? What if it were your baby?"

"But, Papa—"

"Make the call and hire TC, Noah."

Vancy saw Noah cave in. If it had just been her he was up against, Noah might have continued to fight, but Bela's word was still law in the family. "Yes, sir, I will."

"And you," her husband said, turning to her, "I don't care how this matchmaking of yours turns out. I want you to stop being bored and be happy. Your grandchildren are all married, you have new great-grandchildren about to be born, and the curse is broken."

"You forgot something," Vancy said, walking to her husband. Bela was a big man, who, despite his occasional gruffness, had a heart of gold.

"What did I forget?" he asked.

She reached up, grabbed the collar of his flannel shirt, and gave it the smallest of tugs. Obligingly, Bela leaned down, and she kissed his weathered cheek. "You forgot that I have a husband I adore. That makes me happy."

"Well, I'm glad," he blustered.

"And it also makes me want to spread that kind of happiness to others, which is why I'm sure this is going to work out with Eve and TC."

Noah looked upset, but Vancy Bashalde Salo didn't care.

She was sure her two friends were right to suggest she might be good at matchmaking.

And she was sure that Eve and TC were right for each other.

Chapter Three

"Happy Holidays"

TC was less than happy the following Monday when Holiday, Inc., called to say he had another job.

He argued that he'd signed the standard contract because being officially in the company's employ meant he was covered by their liability insurance, but he'd been verbally assured that he'd only be booked for one week at the mall.

They'd countered that the offer had been too good to refuse and he was under contract, so he could take it or get sued.

The last thing TC needed was to be sued.

So he took the job.

He marched into Salo Construction's office annoyed that he'd been pulled away from his computer. He really wanted to be back home with Bert, working on the article. And as much as he had been thinking last week that Nana Vancy's help with Eve might not be such a bad thing, he was pretty sure that this was taking it further than he wanted to go.

So there he was, getting up at the crack of dawn to shovel the driveway in order to be at a job he didn't want at a time he hadn't agreed to.

Letting the air out of his tires was one thing, but making him get up early and miss a second cup of coffee was another thing entirely.

Eve was in the office, surrounded by a stack of files. TC froze, and his ire of the last two hours didn't just fade, it vanished.

"I'm beginning to think that being surrounded by files is your natural habitat," he teased. "The Discovery Channel is probably going to want to make a documentary someday."

"Or maybe National Geographic," she countered with a smile. "Making order out of chaos is my natural habit, so you're close." She stood. "Do you have an appointment?"

"I'm here to see Noah."

"Fine, Mr. Potter. Let me tell him you're here."

Mr. Potter? Uh-oh. It didn't take a bachelor's degree in psychology to realize he was in trouble. "Hey, wait a minute."

Eve paused and turned around. "Yes?"

"Is everything all right?"

"Perfectly fine. And you?"

Ouch. If her tone got any sharper, he'd have to check for cuts. "I'm great."

"Well, then, it appears we're both fine. Now, if you don't mind, let me get Noah so that I can get back to work."

Maybe he'd made a tactical error and should have called her over the weekend. But he didn't want to rush her. And he had planned to call her this week and see if she'd do dinner with him again.

She disappeared into Noah's office, then came back. "Noah's in his office. You can go back."

He thought about saying something, about apologizing for not getting ahold of her over the weekend, but he stopped himself. He suspected that wooing Eve out of her prickles was going to take more time than he had just now. He'd go find out what Noah was up to—as a proxy for Nana Vancy, no doubt—and he'd put a stop to it. Then he'd try cajoling Eve.

He walked into Noah's spartan office, and before he could say anything, Noah stood and threw up his hands. "Don't shoot the messenger."

"That does not sound good."

."Have a seat, TC, and let me explain."

Noah sat back in his chair, and TC took the one on the other side of the desk. "Okay, spill."

"This was so not me. When Papa Bela called Holiday, Inc., at Nana's prompting, and found out you'd signed a contract—"

"At the company's insistence. It put me under their

liability umbrella in case I dropped a kid or got injured picking one up. They said they would only use me for one week. Last week. At the mall. There was never any mention of playing Santa Claus for a construction company."

"But Nana Vancy found out who you were working for and insisted we hire you. And you know Nana . . ." Noah left the sentence hang and looked at TC expectantly.

TC sighed. "Yes, I'm beginning to. I've lived next door to your grandparents for two years, but this last week has been my real introduction to them. But I still don't understand what she hopes to accomplish."

"I'm supposed to give you this shopping list and the company credit card. Well, actually, I'm supposed to give the credit card to Eve. And the two of you are supposed to shop, wrap, and deliver these gifts. You as Santa and Eve as your elf."

"I still don't understand. You could have Eve do the shopping, and you—or, better yet, your grandfather—could play Santa."

"We could. We would. But Nana insisted it had to be you. And Eve."

"Me and Eve. I thought as much." TC nodded as Noah confirmed what both he and Eve had suspected. "And Nana had that mystery doctor's appointment last week that necessitated Eve's picking me up because my four tires were mysteriously flattened overnight. And even dinner that first night, right?"

"Yes."

Though he'd believed that Nana Vancy was setting them up, hearing it put so matter-of-factly still surprised him. "I got that feeling last week, but I don't understand why she's doing it, and, even more, I don't understand why you and your grandfather are going along with it."

"Okay, I'm not proud, but here it is. Nana's bored, TC. It's as simple and complex as that. Ever since the Salo Family Wedding Curse was broken, and all of us have married, she's got nothing left to worry about and try to plan. Her two friends suggested that maybe she'd make a good matchmaker, and . . ." Noah shook his head. "You and Eve are her guinea pigs."

TC took a moment to digest the news.

He waited for the righteous indignation to set in.

The panic at the thought of being trapped.

He waited.

And waited some more.

All he felt was pleased that he was going to get to spend more time with Eve. After all, she hadn't seemed overly thrilled to see him when he came in, but with Nana Vancy's plan, she'd be forced to spend time with him.

So he shrugged. "Okay."

"My grandfather and I are both aghast, but we'd like . . ." Noah's sentence faded as TC's agreement sank in. "Wait a minute. That's it? Okay?"

TC nodded.

"Seriously, I thought you'd be calling my grandmother all kinds of names by now, and, being the good grandson, I'd have to defend her honor, even if I agree she's nuts and her plan's bizarre, and then we'd come to blows. I'd go home with massive bruises—"

"Because I beat you?" TC asked, amused at the obvious thought Noah had given this.

Noah snorted. "No, of course not. Because I won, but *you* put up a great fight before apologizing for slurring my grandmother's name. Anyway, I'd go home with bruises, and Callie would play my nurse."

TC laughed. "You think it would have gone down that way?"

TC was asking about Noah winning. But obviously Noah took the question differently, because he answered, "No. Callie probably would have slugged me and told me not to fight with Nana's neighbors and that Nana Vancy didn't need her honor defended because the entire family recognizes that Nana is occasionally sanity challenged, but we love her anyway."

"I can see your wife doing as much." Callie Salo looked as if she could pack a wallop.

"To be honest, even almost nine months pregnant, Callie wouldn't back down."

TC laughed. "I always thought Callie was a great match for you." He'd heard rumors that before Noah married Callie he'd been engaged to her sister. TC didn't know the sister, but he couldn't imagine a more perfect match for his neighbor than Callie, and he wondered how anyone else had ever missed it.

Even as he heard the thought in his own head, he winced. It sounded far too romantic, and if he'd said it aloud, he'd have deserved any razzing he surely would have taken for it.

"So, when do you want me to start? Us to start?" he corrected.

"Today is fine. You can just tell Eve—"

"Oh, no. I might not argue with this crazy plan, mainly because I like Eve and don't mind spending time with her. And doing community service is always nice. It will add another level to my article. But even though I'm not going to argue with it, I'm also not going to deal with Eve's wrath." He paused and added, "And I anticipate that some wrathfulness will be displayed. I think she's mad at me anyway."

"What did you do?"

"It's what I didn't do. I took her out for dinner last week, then never called."

"Oh."

"But you can't tell your grandmother that. I promised Eve."

"You didn't tell my grandmother, and I didn't promise anything," Noah pointed out.

Noah was studying TC with an intensity that made him uncomfortable. "In my defense, Eve said it wasn't a date and insisted on paying for her own food. But still, she was chilly to the point of frostbite when I came in just now."

"Women." Noah made the word sound like a curse. "If you call too soon, you're needy and clingy. Not soon enough, and you're distant, cold, and out of touch with your feelings. Guys can't win."

"Yeah," TC agreed.

"And why do we have to call anyway? Eve could just as easily have phoned you."

"Yeah," TC repeated. She could have. They'd both been clear it was just dinner, so a call certainly wasn't necessary.

"So, you just take the file out to the reception room and tell Eve I'd like to see her. I'll tell our new in-a-snit office manager that she's to assist you, no ifs, ands, or buts about it. You might have to deal with her mood, but I'm her boss. I don't."

"Thanks, Noah." TC took the file, got up, and started for the door.

"Hey, TC," Noah said, stopping him in his tracks.

TC turned around. "Is there something else?"

"You're sure you don't mind my grandmother's machinations?"

TC double-checked his emotions, weighing them carefully. There was a bit of amusement, knowing this whole situation was absurd. There was some part of him that knew this was going to make for a much better article. And then there was a part of him that, despite the fact that he'd been chased by women for the last year, liked the idea of doing the chasing himself. Especially if the person he was chasing was Eve Allen. Nana Vancy was just pushing him in a direction he wanted to go in anyway.

"No, Noah, I don't mind. But whatever you do, don't tell your grandmother that. If she thinks she has carte blanche . . ." He paused, trying to imagine what Nana Vancy would do then. "I don't even want to think about it."

"I won't tell. Thanks for being such a great sport about this. She was driving us all—Papa Bela, especially—crazy."

"Happy to provide the distraction," TC said. File in hand, he walked back out to the reception area and found Eve once again on the floor, surrounded by her piles of files. "Noah wants to see you."

Eve sighed as she rose. "I'll run back to see what he wants and trust that you can show yourself out."

"Sure," he replied, and he watched her strut down the hall without looking back.

He looked through the file he held. In it were contact names for all three Erie area hospitals. Notes on how much to spend. In addition, there was a standing order for holiday baskets for the employees that they were to pick up and deliver.

There was easily enough work to keep them busy all week and then some.

He'd finished his cursory read-through when Eve came marching back down the hall, her body stiff, her expression anything but pleased.

"Let's get this over with" was all she said as she opened a closet, took out her coat, and started bundling up.

"Wow, your enthusiasm is overwhelming, Eve. Come on, tone it down, or your obvious adulation is going to go to my head," he teased.

"Hey, don't try to pretend that you're any happier about this than I am. Nana Vancy strikes again." She put her arm through one sleeve, and before she could reach back to try to grab the other, TC helped her put it on.

"Come on, there are worse things in this world than being paid to make people's holidays brighter."

She turned around and glared at him before grabbing one of her boots and shoving her foot into it. "Yeah, like what?"

She turned and walked out the door without waiting for his answer.

She was seated in one of the Salo Construction vans when he got in. "The dentist," he said as he put the key into the ignition and started the van.

"Pardon?"

"Going to the dentist is worse than shopping for holiday gifts for other people. And I don't say that as any slur against dentistry. One of my Every American Man articles on jobs was about dentists. They work hard, and most people aren't overly excited about visiting them. But they're committed to clean and healthy teeth."

"I never thought about that."

"It's the sound of the drill. There's nothing worse. . . ."

Eve wasn't sure exactly what she was doing talking dentist drills with TC Potter, aka Tim, aka Timmy Potter.

Oh, she got that Nana Vancy—she'd tried to at least continue thinking of the woman as Mrs. Salo but had failed miserably—was trying to fix her up with TC, but she didn't understand why. And she especially didn't understand why Nana would go to such crazy lengths.

"Yes," she argued, because arguing with TC made her feel as if she wasn't just complacently accepting the situation, "there is something worse than the sound of a dentist's drill."

"Oh? Worse than a dentist's drill?" He sounded skeptical.

"Babies crying. You know, that high-pitched sort of cry that says they're inconsolable. That's worse than any drill."

"Crying in general. That never sounds good," he agreed.

Eve could see that they were inadvertently playing a game. "The sound of your boss' grandmother calling your name."

"The sound of your holiday elf groaning at the thought of spending a day with you."

That last part stopped the game in its tracks. "TC, let's be frank. I'll admit, at first I had a bias against you. Every year since kindergarten you've been on my mind at Christmastime. And not in a flattering way. But you've grown up, and from what I can see, you're a nice enough guy to not only go along with your neighbor's blatant attempts at fixing you up, but you've also apparently forgiven her for slashing your tires in order to further her agenda."

He corrected her. "Nana Vancy didn't slash them. She just let the air out."

"Still, you seem nice enough. But I don't want to date you. Not just you. Anyone. Not for a while, anyway."

"Bad breakup?" he asked as he stopped at a red light.

"The worst breakup. You see, I've always had rules about not dating people I work with. But this one time I broke my rule. And at first it went great. I thought our relationship was great, and so did he, because he was dating not only me but was also seeing my best friend on the side."

"Ouch."

"Yeah, ouch," Eve agreed. "Men suck."

"Not all men are like that. Some guys try to be honest and do what's right."

"Uh, TC, I'm not sure if you truly appreciate the irony of your words. I mean, let's not forget, you don't have the best track record, at least where I'm concerned."

"About that night—I should have told you then—"

Eve interrupted. "No, it's all right. We were kids, and we're older now. Let's just decide to be friends. We'll work together on this project this week and then go our separate ways, no recriminations. I know this isn't your fault."

It wasn't TC's fault; she was positive of that fact. She'd Googled the Salos over the weekend and found the reports from the Salo Family Wedding Curse, not just in the *Erie Times* but in national newspapers as well.

Try as she might, she couldn't recall reading the articles at the time. She must have, but she simply couldn't recall.

Her general feeling as she read the articles and the countless blogs about the curse was that Vancy Bashalde Salo was . . . She searched for a kind word.

Eccentric.

The first fiasco was her namesake, Vancy's, wedding. That led to the first article and granddaughter Vancy's hiding out from the press with Matt Wilde, who'd just inherited twin nephews and needed help. Then there was Noah's almost wedding and his romance with his ex-fiancée's stepsister, Callie. Finally, Dori Salo had ended up with an architect named Bill Hastings who'd pretended to be an interior designer named Carter.

It was all very confusing, but at the heart of all the confusion was Nana Vancy.

Like some old algebraic equation, Eve had it figured out. *Nana Vancy = chaos.*

"We need to decide how to convince Nana Vancy we are not going to be her next match." Although, from the articles, it sounded more as though Nana's grandchildren had found their soul mates despite her meddling, not because of it.

"We'll think of something, but for now let's just enjoy the day. The sun is out, snow is covering the yards and not the streets so much, and the mall shouldn't be too crazy on a Monday morning."

For the next three hours they shopped. They made two trips out to the van to store bags and then went back for more. Eve took charge of the file and neatly noted each gift along with its cost, trying to keep things within the budget Noah had set.

"I don't think Noah meant we had to be that specific on what we spent. It sounded more like a general suggestion."

"I like having boundaries," she informed him.

"And staying within them?"

She nodded. "Life is safer that way. It goes more smoothly if you stay in the lines."

"Sometimes the most exciting things are off the beaten path."

Eve tried not to gag. She'd had more than enough off-the-beaten-path this past year to last her a lifetime.

A bit of quiet and order—that's all she wanted. It didn't seem like too much to ask. "Well, it's good that we're thwarting Nana's matchmaking plans, because it's apparent we have very different ideas on things."

Eve realized how prim that sounded and said, "Sorry."

TC seemed unfazed. "No problem. Let's get some lunch."

"No, if we power through, we can get this done in another hour or so. I'll just grab something on the way back to work."

"Or we could stop and have lunch before my stomach eats itself."

She laughed. Try as she might, it was hard to maintain a professional distance from TC. He was nice. Much nicer than he was in her memories of ninth grade and kindergarten.

"Fine," she said. "I don't want to be responsible for your stomach's eating itself."

They stopped at the food court, and Eve went straight for the Chinese food. She loved vegetable lo mein and came back with a heaping plateful. TC had a burger.

"So, after we're done eating, we'll finish the shopping. Then tomorrow I'll set up the meeting room as command central, and we'll wrap and package. We won't have to worry about anything else until Friday, when we deliver everything. Then we're done. It will only tie up two more days this week—"

"Sorry, check the list. We're tied up every day.

Tuesday we wrap. Wednesday we have appointments at two of the hospitals, Thursday at the other, then Friday it's the employees. We're doing the hospitals as Santa and his elf. Oh, and Thursday we're doing some promo shots as Santa and his elf. The Salos are doing a calendar for next year, and we're December."

"That's not in the file." Eve had read through everything, and she was sure.

"Yes, it is. On the back of the file itself."

Eve turned the manila flap and looked. "The whole week? Nana Vancy set it up so we're together every day for the whole week?"

"Hey, all you have to do is keep reminding yourself that it could be worse."

"Yeah, crying babies and dentist drills."

TC didn't seem to take offense. As a matter of fact, he laughed. "See? You're catching on."

And despite the fact that TC Potter had once ruined her Christmas by telling her there was no real Santa Claus, and then ruined a second Christmas by standing her up for the holiday formal, she had to admit, there were worse things than spending a week in his company.

"Okay, so I'm yours . . . for the week."

Chapter Four

"O Christmas Tree"

The following day TC had to admit that what Nana Vancy lacked in subtlety, she made up for with flash.

He and Eve walked into Salo Construction's conference room, where they'd stored the bags of gifts the day before. It had been a normal-looking, utilitarian meeting room then, with a long table and plenty of chairs. The only decorations were framed photos of Salo Construction projects, including Hazard Hills, Dori's personal pet project.

Today it looked as if one of Santa's more certifiable elves had been let loose.

"Nana Vancy," they both muttered as they took in the redesign.

Pine garland hung from window frames and the backs of chairs, bows punctuating every few feet of greenery. The framed pictures had been taken down and wrapped as if they were presents, then put back into place.

In a corner was a tree covered with lights, candy canes, and more bows.

But it was the ceiling that was Nana Vancy's pièce de résistance.

"I think there must be a hundred bunches of mistletoe up there," Eve muttered.

"More, maybe." TC stared up at the once-white ceiling tiles that were now covered with bits of the kiss-inspiring greenery. "I don't suppose you want to give it a try?"

Eve snorted her response.

TC expected to feel relieved; instead, he felt disappointed. After a year of dodging women's advances, of reading disturbing and strange letters of proposal, of feeling objectified, TC was finding himself wishing that Eve was a little awed by him. He wasn't sure why, but he wanted her to want him. He realized he was attracted to her in a way he'd thought he'd forgotten.

He liked that she was up-front about her feelings.

He liked that when she relaxed and let her guard down, she was a lot of fun.

He liked that she didn't mind Bert's drool.

And he really liked that she was a tall woman who could almost look him in the eye.

Well, he liked that part most of the time, but as she stood there, staring at him with an expression that said she was pretty sure he was crazier than Nana Vancy, that part slipped down a notch on his things-I-like-about-Eve list.

He hadn't really known he had such a list until that moment, but he realized, other than that one slip, the list was growing.

"Let's get started," Eve said.

It was after eleven when Noah poked his head into the meeting room. "What on earth . . . ?" he muttered as he took in the decorations. "It wasn't me."

"We didn't think it was," Eve assured her boss, who looked almost embarrassed.

TC pointed toward the ceiling. "I assume that wasn't you, either?"

"I'm going to kill her," Noah said, with more oomph to his vow this time. "We were all trying to humor her, but this is a case of giving an inch and her taking a mile . . . or a ceiling, as the case may be."

"Noah, don't worry." Eve pulled out the wrapping paper and started on a package. "I've decided that I'm just going to consider your grandmother's matchmaking attempts amusing. I mean, it's not as if I find TC attractive, so there really are no worries."

Eve's offhand comment about his unattractiveness set TC's teeth on edge. "Hey—"

"Sorry," she said, interrupting him. "I don't mean you're not attractive. I'm sure you are. I mean, women all over the country have spent the last year hitting on you, and *Famous Magazine* obviously felt you were attractive enough to be one of their most eligible bachelors. It's just that I don't see you that way."

TC felt a warm glow as Eve spouted off more information than he'd ever given her. She had to have looked him up.

And why would she do that if she wasn't interested?

But then her comment about not seeing him *that way* hit.

"Why not?" Noah and TC asked in unison.

Eve frowned at both of them, but TC didn't care. He wanted answers.

"Well, for starters, I want something more than a pretty face in a man I'm interested in."

TC waved a hand. "Award-winning writer. That must indicate there's something more than a pretty face about me."

"Well, I want more than intellect too. I want someone who has a sense of humor, someone who sweeps me off my feet. And most important, I want someone I can trust." She frowned as she listed that last requirement.

TC wanted to kick her ex in the . . .

He tried to distract himself from what he envisioned doing to the guy who'd hurt Eve by asking, "You don't think I can do those things? Be those things?"

"I think you broke my heart in kindergarten when you told me there was no Santa Claus, and again when you stood me up. I'm not really open to a third time."

"He stood you up?" Noah asked.

TC had forgotten that Eve's boss was still here.

"Back in ninth grade," he answered. He might have told Eve why if they were alone, but he was once again suddenly aware of the fact that Noah Salo was there. So all he said was, "I'd like to think I've grown since then."

"Maybe, but really, TC, it doesn't matter if you have. I'm not interested." She curled some ribbon on the present she'd been working on.

"Oh." He didn't know what else to say to her beyond that, so he turned to Noah. "We're going to work for a while, then take lunch, if that's okay."

"Yeah, it's fine. And I'm going to apologize to both of you. I know this is a pain, but it's been months since Nana's been this happy. So, if you don't mind just finishing out the week . . ."

"No, of course we don't mind," Eve said. "We might not be interested in each other the way your grandmother wants us to be, but that doesn't mean I don't like TC. He's an enjoyable companion, and I'm sure passing out the presents will be fun. Plus, when I took this job, your grandfather assured me I'd be more than a glorified receptionist. I'd be managing the office and dealing with all sorts of unusual circumstances. Of course, I didn't realize they'd be quite this unusual, but still . . ." She shrugged.

That's all that Noah needed. "Great. I'm going to leave in a bit, and I'll be out of the office this afternoon. When you leave for lunch, just lock up, okay?"

"What if someone comes while we're both gone?"

"I don't have any appointments, and most people, knowing the nature of our business, don't just drop in. If they do, they'll drop back when they see the OUT TO LUNCH sign. It's in the window to the right of the door. Take as long as you want for lunch—we owe you a lot more than a long lunch. I'll see you in the morning."

"Fine. See you then, Noah." Eve went back to her ribbons.

"Later, Salo," TC said. The moment Eve's boss was gone, TC forgot about him. His mind was too filled with other thoughts. Thoughts that seemed to center around Eve.

After a year of dodging women's attentions, he'd found a woman he'd like to attract . . . and she had just made it perfectly clear she wasn't interested.

The irony of the situation didn't escape him.

And TC Potter, award-winning writer, a man who prided himself on his keen insights into what made people tick, didn't have a clue what to do about it.

Nana Vancy was stirring a pot of soup as she and the other Salo girls listened to her namesake and granddaughter Vancy's newest tale of the kids' fiascos. ". . . and that's when I walked in and found that Chris and Ricky had tied Fred to a chair and were lacing belts to the back of the chair, telling her they were going to give her an elevator ride off—"

"Nana, this has to stop," Noah said as he burst into the kitchen and interrupted his sister.

"Noah, that was rude," his wife, Callie, scolded. She waddled toward him and kissed his cheek, then turned and asked, "So what did you do now, Nana?"

"Nothing. I didn't do anything wrong." Why on earth did her family always get so upset? She was doing something nice, not committing a crime.

"Nana . . ." Dori's voice had a hint of warning in it.

"Well, maybe I decorated the conference room a little, to put TC and Eve in the proper mood, *lanyunoka.*" She had to admit, the mistletoe was a flash of brilliance. She'd enlisted Annabelle and Isabel's help with the decorations, and they'd worked for hours on it.

They'd all three agreed that the room was quite the romantic place when they were finished.

She could almost imagine TC and Eve falling in love under the mistletoe.

"It didn't work," Noah assured her.

"No kissing under the mistletoe?" she asked, disappointment flooding her system.

"None," he assured her. "Just some present-wrapping."

"Well, they still have the rest of the week together." She was optimistic, and with good reason. She'd believed that she would break the Salo Family Wedding Curse, and she had. It was broken, her grandchildren were all happily married, and she was sure her luck would hold out. Eve and TC were meant to be together. She could feel it in her very Hungarian bones.

She wasn't sure why she was so sure. She'd decided to find someone for Eve before she'd even met the girl. And TC had been a convenient choice. After all, what girl wouldn't fall in love with one of the country's most eligible bachelors? He was smart, funny, and a very nice man.

Eve could do worse.

As if he'd heard her thoughts, Noah said, "Eve made it clear she wasn't even remotely interested in TC Potter. And it seems they knew each other before you introduced them. He stood her up in the past. She's not the kind of woman who would easily forget something like that."

"Oh." Nana Vancy was impressed. Her Noah was turning out to be quite the detective.

And TC and Eve knew each other in the past?

Somehow she must have sensed that.

It had to be her Hungarian roots.

Just as she'd always known that words had power, she had also always sincerely believed that some people were more intuitive than others. That they could sense things.

She'd just never really believed she was one of those people.

Now she knew for sure that she was, that she'd sensed that TC and Eve were meant to be together before she really could have known it. Clearly she was amazingly gifted and would trust her instincts even more in the future.

"Thank you, Noah. That was helpful information."

"Nana, what are you going to do?" Noah sounded worried.

"Now, Noah, don't you fret. . . ."

"Yes, Noah," Callie said. "Your grandmother has a way of making things happen. I'm sure, if this thing between TC and Eve is meant to be—"

"There is no *if,*" Vancy assured Callie. As each minute ticked by, Vancy Bashalde Salo felt more and more convinced that her second sight was real.

"There you go," Dori said. "There was a time I might have scoffed, but . . ." She shrugged.

"We're here to help you, Nana," her granddaughter, Vancy, said.

"Yes, we're with you," Callie agreed.

Noah groaned. "Nana, what have you done to them?"

"Nothing. Women just understand things quicker than men do, and the girls understand that TC and Eve are meant to be together. I don't know how I know it, but I do. They just need a little help."

He groaned even louder. "Nana . . ." His voice had a world of warning in it.

"Don't worry. It will all work out."

Vancy Bashalde Salo would see to it.

Chapter Five

"Jingle Bells"

"**D**on't worry, it will all work out," TC called through the bathroom door on Wednesday.

Eve was pretty sure he was wrong. Oh, yesterday had gone better than she'd thought it would. They'd wrapped gifts and had a lovely lunch. TC was a fun companion after all. If Nana Vancy hadn't been trying to set them up, she'd have enjoyed spending platonic, non-dating time with him.

But he was so wrong about this. She looked down, sure she must have been imagining how bad it was, but rather than dissuading her, the second look convinced her. It was that bad.

"Come on, Eve."

"I don't think so. Wild reindeer and all that," she assured him through the door—the door she intended to keep locked until she changed back into her own clothes.

There was nothing in her job description about wearing things like this.

"Come out and let me see. I'll let you see mine if you let me see yours."

Despite the horribleness of her outfit, she laughed. "No way."

"Nana Vancy wouldn't have given you an outfit that was too risqué."

"I didn't say anything about its being risqué. I simply said there was no way I was going to be seen in public wearing this."

She gazed into the bathroom mirror and was thankful that it wasn't a full-length one. Because what she could see from her waist up was bad enough. The striped tights would have only magnified the effect.

"Come on, Eve. It's the holiday season, and these are sick kids in a hospital. If your outfit looks a bit ridiculous, maybe it will make them smile, and anything that can make a sick child smile is a good thing."

She admitted defeat, and, after one more horrifying glance in the mirror, she opened the bathroom door and found Santa Claus waiting for her.

TC took in her outfit, his blue eyes peeping over his Santa glasses, slowly moving from her red-and-white-striped tights-covered legs to her frilly green-and-white checked dress to her white-eyelet apron . . . and right up to her holly-covered bonnet.

"I feel as if Christmas just barfed all over me," she complained. "At least you look like a normal Santa. Me? I'm a freakish elf. I'm that elf who, when she was in high school, never had the current elf fashions and ended up borrowing her mother elf's stuff. Yep, I'm the pariah elf dressed in outdated Mom-Elf clothes. I'm sure none of the other little elves sat with me at lunch. I probably was the last elf picked for the elf gym teams."

"I'd have sat with you." There was sincerity in TC's words, even if he was still grinning.

"You're Santa Claus. Santa is the epitome of kindness. The other elves, not so much. And can you imagine what the kids will do when they see this getup?"

"Hey, if they laugh, you'll know you gave them a break from their misery."

"When you put it that way—again—how can I not do it?"

"So, let's go."

TC picked up a bag they'd stuffed with gifts. Eve had labeled them with a carefully coded system: blue for boys over ten; brown for boys under ten but not toddlers; toddler boys were red. . . .

"This thing weighs a ton," TC complained as he trudged to the van with it.

"There are, unfortunately, a lot of kids in the hospital."

The trip didn't take long, and Eve was glad that TC was content to ride in silence.

She needed to think.

Thinking had become increasingly difficult with TC around.

She wasn't sure why.

They had a history together, and not one filled with pleasant memories. At least not for her. Her jokes about being the freakish elf hit sort of close to home.

She'd been one of those awkward kids in school. Tall and gangly. Some tall kids excelled at sports. She, unfortunately, had had the height but not the coordination. So she'd fallen into her books. In books she could become any character. She could become everything she wasn't. Graceful. Beautiful.

She looked down at her less-than-stellar outfit. In books she dressed well too.

It was here, in the real world, that she messed up.

She chose boyfriends who cheated with friends who were more beautiful. She'd had so many bad boyfriends, she no longer trusted her own judgment.

She glanced at TC.

No, liking him was out of the question.

So she wasn't going to.

End of discussion, even if she was only discussing it with herself.

Three hours later, TC was entranced by watching Eve with the kids.

She was wearing the most ridiculous elf costume ever. It made him glad he got to be Santa.

She'd been so upset about it at first, but somewhere along the line she'd forgotten about the monstrosity of the outfit and started concentrating on the kids.

And Eve with the kids was an amazing thing to behold.

She didn't see the wires or the tubes, the shaved heads or frail bodies. She simply saw the kids.

Right now, she was entertaining three little girls who were sharing a room.

Eve goofed around and laughed with them. And, sitting on the edge of a bed, she began reciting a Christmas poem.

". . . then Santa sneezed, ha, ha, ha choo,

and with a hanky his nose he blew.

He didn't glance left or right

But reached into his bag and pulled out a . . ."

She paused to mime reaching into a huge bag, then slowly, slowly pulling something out of it. Something big. Something that pulled her arm toward the ceiling.

". . . a kite!" one of the girls called out.

Eve nodded. ". . . a kite." She continued with the poem.

"It lifted dear Santa clear off the floor,

And flew dear Santa right toward the door.

The children forgot they were safely hid,

And ran toward him, laughing, as they slid.

The kids grabbed his coat and pulled him to the floor.

Dear Santa, please stay, and the milk we'll pour.

Mom made the treats. We'll have them now.

"Dear Santa, please stay . . ."

Eve beckoned TC toward the group and continued reciting.

"Dear Santa, please stay, and tell us how,

You fly at night so near and far,

Do you follow Rudolph, or follow a star?"

She paused, the poem obviously finished. "So, Santa, tell us how you manage Christmas Eve. I mean, visiting the hospital a couple of weeks before Christmas must seem like a cakewalk compared to what you do on Christmas Eve."

"Ho! Ho! Ho! Well, Evey Elf, you're right," TC said in his best jovial Santa voice. "Christmas Eve is a very busy night. But—Ho! Ho! Ho!—good old Santa enjoys days like this a lot. It's nice to visit the children and say hi, rather than creeping in and out of their houses at night."

For the next twenty minutes the kids asked questions, and he tried his best to answer. His favorite food was hot cocoa. When a little girl named Madi pointed out that cocoa wasn't a food but rather a drink, he corrected his answer to, "The marshmallows."

The kids loved having an audience and kept up the questions, and TC was congratulating himself on being quick with his responses, when the little girl named Sarah asked, "Hey, Evey Elf, how come you're so tall? I mean, wow, you're taller than my daddy, and he's very tall."

TC held his breath, not sure how Eve would handle the question, but he should have known by now that she would.

"Well, unlike some of the other elves at the North Pole, I eat my vegetables every day and always drink my milk."

"Yeah, my mom says you gotta do that to get big and strong," a little girl named Regan said.

"Your mom is right," Eve assured her.

They passed out the presents to the trio and had started for the next room when Madi ran after them in the hallway. "Hey, I know there's no such thing as Santa Claus, but I didn't tell the littler kids."

The girl couldn't be more than six or seven, but she sounded so much older.

"I just wanted to say thanks," she continued. "They've been sort of grumpy, what with being stuck in here and missing out on school parties and stuff."

Eve sank down on one knee and looked the dark-haired little girl in the eye. "You're right that this isn't the real Santa Claus. He's just helping out the real Santa. There are a lot of hospitals and a lot of sick kids to visit, and even as magical as Santa is, he needs some help."

Madi scoffed. "There's no real Santa."

"Well, I was in kindergarten when someone told me that, and for a few years I was brokenhearted," Eve said softly. "It was as if someone had stolen my best friend. Christmas had always been my favorite holiday, but suddenly I hated it. I felt as if everyone had lied to me, and even as a little girl, I hated being lied to."

"Yeah, it took a long time for Mom to tell me I was sick. I was mad for a while too, but then I saw her crying, and I figured out she just wanted to keep me from gettin' scared like her."

"Yes. And I was mad too for a long time. But when I was in fourth grade, my dad was laid off from his job, and we didn't have a lot of money for presents. I told my mom and dad not to worry about it, that I didn't need presents. My mom said that I was right, that they couldn't afford gifts, but that Santa always could." Eve's voice broke, and she paused a moment, then continued. "Christmas morning came, and there were all these packages under the tree for me. I couldn't figure out how it happened."

"Don't tell me it was Santa," Madi scoffed.

"No. Turns out my dad sold his fancy car and bought us this old clunker of a van. They used the money to pay some of the bills but took some of it to buy me Christmas presents. There was one very small box that had a charm in it. It was a bird in a tree. I didn't get it at first, but it was a partridge in a pear tree, like the song?"

Madi nodded.

"Well, I wear it every holiday season." Eve reached down her collar and pulled out a chain and the small partridge-in-a-pear-tree charm. "I wear it to remind myself there *is* a Santa Claus. He just doesn't come down a chimney or wear a red suit. He's everyone who tries to do something nice for someone else. He's my mom and dad, taking money they needed for themselves and buying me presents. He's today's Santa, TC, who took time to come to the hospital and bring a few smiles to you guys."

"I get it," Madi said. "And Santa is an elf named Evey who wears an ugly bird in a tree to remember that her parents love her."

"Yeah, that's right."

Madi hugged her. "I'll remember that, and maybe I'll be Santa Claus this year too," she said softly into Eve's ear.

"Merry Christmas, Madi," Eve murmured back.

For a moment TC just stood there, watching Eve and the little girl whose illness had made her grow up too soon. And as Eve rose, he didn't see the hideous elf costume Nana Vancy had left for her to wear. He saw the most beautiful woman he'd ever met.

He felt a flood of emotion so huge, he didn't know what to do with it all.

Madi went back into her hospital room, and TC still stood there, looking at Eve. "I'm sorry," he finally said.

"For what?"

For making you doubt there was a Santa Claus all those years ago. I was an obnoxious kindergartner."

Eve smiled. "Yeah, you were, but I eventually figured it out."

"I thought you didn't like Christmas."

"Sometimes I still forget that I love it . . . but as of right now I've remembered all over again. Bad breakups can't take away the holiday's magic."

TC looked up and down the hallway and spotted what he was looking for a few doors up.

He walked toward his goal, Eve following, and when they reached the mistletoe, he turned around and, before she could protest, he kissed her.

One full-on, lips-to-lips kiss.

Eve pulled back and looked at him as if he'd grown a third eye. "What was that for?"

"That was because you are the most beautiful woman I've ever met, and if I didn't kiss you, I'd have gone crazy."

"Well, it didn't work." She wiped at her lips as if he had Santa cooties. "You are quite certifiably crazy. So, let's forget what just happened and go finish delivering our gifts."

"Whatever you say, Evey Elf."

And as TC followed her down the hall, he whistled "Jingle Bells" because it was a happy tune and it gave all those emotions whirling in the pit of his stomach an outlet.

Later, when he was alone and had some distance, he'd figure out just what all those emotions were.

And just what he was going to do about them.

On Friday, Eve was wishing that TC would stop staring at her. She didn't need to turn around and look to know that he was doing it again. She could almost feel his eyes boring holes into her back.

"Cut it out," she called over her shoulder.

"What?" he asked, the picture of innocence.

She didn't respond because he knew what. And she knew what. And she was done. "Let's get this last delivery loaded, and then you can go your way and I'll go mine."

She entered the conference room and looked at the piles of packages. They were much smaller than they had been on. Wednesday when they'd started delivering.

"Or?" he said slowly.

"Or, what?"

"Or after we finish this delivery, you'll go to dinner with me."

She snorted. "I can't."

"Can't or won't?" he pressed.

TC Potter had been absolutely crazy since Wednesday and that first hospital visit. He'd been giving her goo-goo looks and had tried to kiss her a couple more times, but now that she was on the lookout, she'd dodged those kisses quite effectively.

Eve wasn't sure what had happened, why he was acting like this, and she hadn't figured out how to fix it. So she tried again. "Listen, TC, it's almost the new year, and I've made a few early resolutions."

"Such as?"

"I'm taking some time off from men. As a matter of

fact, after wearing this outfit for days, I'm about as Christmas-ed out as I can get."

"I like the outfit."

She snorted her response.

"And I like you," he said in another example of gooey sentimentality. "Say you'll have dinner with me."

"No."

"All right."

He'd given up way too easily. Eve eyed him suspiciously. "TC, what are you thinking?"

"I'm thinking that it's been nice seeing you again, and I've enjoyed spending time with you this week, but you're right—it's best we just let things end here."

She sighed with relief. "I'm glad you're finally being sensible."

"Of course, Nana Vancy asked me to call her after we finished today. I'm sure she's going to grill me on the two of us and how things went this week. I'll have to tell her that her plan didn't work."

"Well, she should probably know. It'd be cruel to keep her hoping. I still don't understand why she was setting us up. She doesn't even know me."

"I can answer that," Noah said as he entered the conference room. "She's bored."

"Pardon?" Eve asked.

"She's bored, and that boredom has led to her current delusions of having romantic ESP. All of this"—he waved a hand at the overly decorated room and pointed specifically toward the ceiling of mistletoe—"is because she's convinced that not only did she have the ability to curse our family and then break the curse, but that she also has some uncanny ability to matchmake. She vowed that the two of you would be in love by Christmas, and she's rather determined."

"She's your grandmother—undetermine her," Eve said.

"I wish I could, but the family would do me in. She's got all the girls on her side, and two of them are pregnant, Eve. All of us know better than to mess with a pregnant woman—especially when by 'all of us' I mean me, and one of those pregnant women is my wife."

"Why would your sisters and wife help your grandmother with this crazy scheme?" Eve asked.

"That's easy. Love. Nana's been happier this week than she's been since right after Dori's wedding. And they all love her and love that she's happy."

"Noah, I know you're my boss, but, really, this was never in my job description . . . ," she began, expecting TC to back her up.

TC edged closer to Noah, who said, "They're going to ask me, the whole family, how things are going between the two of you. I'm afraid that if Nana's not convinced that this is working, she's going to up the ante."

"How? How could she do anything more? She's hired TC and forced him—"

"There was no force," TC said.

When she gave him a look, he clarified, "Well, not really."

"I have no clue what my grandmother will do," Noah said, "but Vancy, Dori, and even Callie are helping her. And if there's anything worse than a matchmaking grandmother, it's a matchmaking grandmother with three newly married women assisting her."

"So, lie," Eve said, feeling rather desperate. "Tell them that TC and I are madly in love, and all they have to do is back off and allow our romance to blossom."

"No," TC said. "If Noah tries to lie, I'll tell Nana Vancy the truth myself."

Had the entire world gone mad? "Why, TC?"

"Because I want you to agree have dinner with me."

"This is crazy. It's coercion. Blackmail, even."

"Maybe," TC said, looking totally unrepentant. "But, come on, we worked hard all week, and you have to eat, so tell me yes."

Noah looked surprised, and Eve knew that her own expression probably reflected even more surprise than his. What was TC up to?

"The last time you asked me out, you stood me up."

"Come out to dinner with me tonight, and I'll explain. There is an explanation. Not an excuse, but a reason," he said cryptically.

Eve stared from one crazy man to the other. "Fine. But that's it. I'll go out with you, and Noah has to tell his grandmother we're both deliriously happy so she'll leave us alone." She turned to Noah. "Do you promise?"

"Sure, I swear." He made a scout's sign.

Eve just shook her head. "Fine. Dinner. Then that's it."

"Fine."

TC wore an expression that Eve didn't quite understand. An expression that said he was up to something, but, for the life of her, she couldn't figure out what it could be.

He gave Noah a look she couldn't quite decipher either, and Eve decided not to even try. She'd have one more dinner with this crazy man and then quietly ignore whatever new schemes Nana Vancy came up with.

Maybe she'd tell the Salo matriarch that she'd eloped over the holidays with her ex. If she was married, that would certainly make Nana stop her matchmaking attempts . . . wouldn't it?

Chapter Six

"Christmas in Killarney"

"You're not talking," TC said as they sat near the fireplace at Molly Brannigan's, an Irish pub on State Street. A band on the other side of the fireplace played holiday music.

"What do you want me to say, TC? Thanks for blackmailing me into having a meal with you?" Eve wasn't even trying to hide her frustration at this obvious ploy. She couldn't figure out what TC was up to.

From her Google search, she knew that not only was TC one of the country's most eligible bachelors, but women all across the country had spent the past year trying to convince him that he should relinquish his title—both the *eligible* and the *bachelor* parts.

"Fine. I wanted to bring you out to apologize," he said.

"Apologize for what?" She refused to be lulled by the fact that Molly Brannigan's was one of her favorite restaurants in town. She wasn't going to let the fact that she would soon be eating the establishment's mouthwatering fish-and-chips sway her. TC was up to something. She could sense it.

He shook his head, and it reminded her of the gesture her father had often made when she was in her teens and being unreasonable. Well, she wasn't in her teens now, and being a bit churlish after being blackmailed into dinner wasn't the least unreasonable.

TC stopped shaking his head and said, "I want to apologize for ninth grade. For standing you up. I'm sorry."

"It was a long time ago. I'm more than over it."

"Listen, I should have apologized at the time, but, Eve, there was a lot going on, and I didn't think, and by the time I realized what I'd done, you were pissed, and it just seemed easier to let things stand."

"Wow, TC, that was an eloquent monologue that said absolutely nothing new." She took a wedge of fried pita and dunked it into warm dip.

"My father had a heart attack the day of the dance. I was at the hospital, and the last thing on my mind was our date, which had been the biggest thing on my mind for weeks before that."

"Oh." Eve went from righteous indignation to feeling small and petty in an eye-blink. She swallowed the bite of bread, which promptly lodged in her throat in a way that had nothing to do with the cooking and everything to do with her guilt. "I'm sorry."

"That's not why I told you. I just wanted you to understand that it was never that I wasn't interested; it was that I was young and didn't handle it right. I tried to talk to you afterward, but you made it clear you weren't interested, and I let it go. That was my mistake. One I didn't want to make again. Which is why I blackmailed you into coming to dinner."

"That's not fair," Eve said. His confession had taken away her reason for being upset over not just the dinner blackmail but about the dance so many years ago.

"I tried to be fair back in high school and just let you go. Dad wasn't able to work for months, and I took an extra job to help make ends meet. I didn't have time for dating or anything else, anyway. I thought it was easier to just let you be pissed at me. I don't want to be 'fair' or take the 'easy' way out this time. I want to see you."

"Why?" And this was the crux of her puzzlement. TC Potter could have any woman he wanted, so why her?

"Because . . ." He paused. "I don't know. I just know that I've enjoyed getting to know you again. I had a blast this week."

"But, TC, I'm not looking for any kind of relationship. I'm on a man hiatus. I need to get my life back into order. I want to concentrate on my new job. I want to concentrate on me."

"I'm not saying you have to concentrate on me. I'm just saying that I'd like to see you."

"And I'm saying no. I'm sorry for all those years of ill-will I directed at you. That had to have been a tough time for you and your entire family. But, that being said, I still don't want to get involved."

The waitress came and brought their meals.

"Let's just have a nice evening. Two old friends hanging out with no expectation of anything more. And then we'll go our separate ways."

"Sure, whatever you say, Eve."

TC sounded sincere and looked as much as he dove into the biggest piece of fish she'd ever seen. But there was something in his eyes that made her nervous. A glint. It reminded her of when he was in kindergarten and broke the news that there was no Santa Claus.

It was a look that said trouble.

Yet she couldn't fault him as they had their meal. He was friendly and chatty, exactly what an old friend would be.

When they finished, and he drove her home, TC put the car into Park and turned off the ignition.

"You don't have to do that. I'll just run inside." She had her hand on the door handle. "Thanks, TC. Really. It was great seeing you again and putting our old animosity to rest."

"It was never *our* animosity, Eve. It was yours."

"Well, then, it was good putting that behind me.

Have a great holiday." She pulled on the handle with her right hand, even as TC grabbed her left.

"Before you go . . . ," he said.

"Yes?"

He gave a tug and pulled her his way.

Eve knew what was coming. She still had her hand on the door handle and could have pulled back and resisted.

She could have just said no.

Instead, she let him kiss her.

She didn't exactly kiss him back.

At least, she didn't think she did.

Okay, so there might have been a bit of softening against him, a moment of her kissing him, but it was over in an instant, and she pulled back. She didn't say anything. Not *how dare you*. Not *that wasn't fair*.

Not anything.

She merely opened the door, grabbed her purse, and got out of his truck.

"Good-bye, TC."

And that was that.

Eve Allen was done with TC Potter.

And she was going to get back to her organized life.

She had stepped outside the bounds of her rules once before, and look how that had turned out. She wasn't going to do it again. She was going to concentrate on getting herself back into order.

The thought should have brought her comfort. But

as she unlocked her front door and glanced behind her at TC's truck pulling out of her driveway, she felt something other than comfort. She wasn't sure what it was, exactly.

But she had the slightest suspicion it might be regret.

". . . and so I took her out to dinner," TC told Nana Vancy the next afternoon. He'd been making a half-hearted attempt at decorating for Christmas. He'd even put a Christmas CD in the player, but it didn't put him in the mood.

Nana Vancy had stopped in on the pretense of borrowing a cup of sugar, but TC had filled her in on his own.

Maybe she'd have some idea how to win Eve over. Of course, any idea Nana Vancy had was bound to be a bit outside the norm. But he was desperate enough to try anything.

"And you kissed her?" his neighbor asked.

Bert came and fell over onto TC's feet and immediately started to snore.

He leaned over and patted the dog's head. "Yes. I've kissed her a couple of times now, and when I kissed her good-bye last night, I think she kissed me back. And that's a good sign. But, Nana Vancy, she said we were through after dinner. We've delivered all Salo's gifts, and my week of working for you all is over. There's no reason for me to be hanging around next week."

"And that's why you came to me? Looking for an excuse to be near her?"

"Well, let's be honest, you came over here for some sugar—sugar that I suspect you don't really need."

She smiled an unrepentant smile and admitted, "I don't. But I'd barely asked when you started confessing, so you must want my help."

TC was embarrassed to admit it, but he did. "Yes, that's exactly what I want. Some idea on how to reach her. Eve was hurt in the past—I know it, even if she didn't tell me. I need her to see that I'd never hurt her. I need something big. Something that will melt her heart."

"You need a plan."

"Deck the Halls" started playing on the CD.

"Yes. And who better to ask advice from than the lady who let the air out of my tires and started this whole thing?"

"You need a plan because you care for Eve?" she asked. "Because I don't want to help you if all you're planning to do is toy with her affections."

"Yes, I care for her. There was this moment, this unguarded moment at the hospital, when she was talking to one of the kids . . ." He didn't know how to describe that moment with Madi in the hall, so he shrugged. "I don't know how to define it. *Caring* doesn't sound quite right, but I do. I do care."

"Did I ever tell you how I fell in love with my Bela?"

"No."

"I was six, and he was going fishing with the big boys, and I begged to go as well. They all said no, that I was a girl and couldn't go. I told them my father was mayor of Erdely, and I could do anything I wanted. Bela leaned down and said, 'Vancy, your father's job is because of what he did, and what you're doing is because of who you are. You're being a spoiled brat, and no one wants to be with someone like that.'"

"Ow," TC said.

"Yes. And as I watched all the big boys going down the road with their fishing poles slung over their shoulders, I hated Bela Salo. I was Vancy Bashalde, and my father was mayor. He doted on me and let me have everything I wanted. I'd just go and tell him—"

She paused in the middle of a rousing string of fa-la-la's from his Christmas CD.

Her cheeks turned a bright pink. "Even after all these years, I'm embarrassed to remember what a brat I was indeed. But Bela had cared enough about me to tell me the truth of it. And that's where my love began. I knew I could always trust my Bela to tell me the truth. I only forgot to believe once, when I thought he'd deserted me, and I started the curse. . . ." She shook her head. "I didn't ever make that mistake again."

"Eve said she'd broken up with her ex because he cheated on her. I wish I could find a way to make her believe in me."

"TC, I stopped being a brat after that fishing incident. I always helped the boys clean the fish they caught, and I helped them find the perfect saplings for new poles, and eventually, because I stopped bugging them but remained helpful and persistent, they invited me fishing. After that, I always went with them. Bela still takes me fishing in the summers."

"I don't want to wait until summer to take her fishing."

"Deck the Halls" gave way to "The Twelve Days of Christmas."

"That's not what I'm saying. I'm saying, be persistent." She was quiet for a moment, and she cocked her head, as if listening to something. She nodded and said, "It's Christmastime, and I have an idea."

TC knew that those words—*I have an idea*—when uttered by Nana Vancy should strike abject terror into the heart of any rational man. But TC had discovered that when it came to Eve Allen, he wasn't rational in the least.

"Okay, tell me what to do," he said.

Chapter Seven

". . . A Partridge in a Pear Tree."

Eve was curled under the quilt watching *A Year Without a Santa Claus* for the millionth time.

Normally it was one of the highlights of her holiday, but this year, every time Santa came on and ho-ho-ho-ed, all she could think about was TC Potter.

"Blue Christmas" started playing as a little girl wrote a letter to Santa outlining how much she'd miss him this Christmas. Eve felt tears well up in her eyes.

The tears had everything to do with missing her parents and nothing at all to do with missing TC.

Maybe she shouldn't have been so quick to tell her parents their leaving over the holidays wouldn't bother her.

Maybe she still had a bit more Christmas spirit than she'd thought she did.

The doorbell rang, interrupting the song. She pressed pause on her DVD player's remote and wiped her eyes as she got up and hurried to the door.

She peeked out and saw . . . nothing.

She opened the door and saw a small package wrapped in red paper hanging from her mailbox's hooks.

It had her name on it.

She scanned the street but didn't see anyone, and though there was plenty of snow on the grass, the sidewalks were bare, so there weren't even footprints.

She took the box into the house, and, once the door was closed, she opened the envelope attached to it. "I saw these and thought of you. May you always remember that the spirit of Santa Claus lives in all of us."

Inside were two hideously ugly earrings. A pair of birds in trees.

She pulled her necklace out, and while they didn't match perfectly, the were close.

Who on earth could have sent them to her?

She fingered the gold hooks and studied the earrings.

Her parents knew what the necklace meant to her, but she'd never told the story to anyone else . . . except the little girl, Madi.

And TC had been there.

She picked up the phone and dialed his cell's number.

"Merry Christmas." He sounded slightly breathless.

As if he'd been running.

Eve had suspected that the earrings were from him. Now she knew. "Thank you."

"For what?" he asked, sounding innocent. Far too innocent. Which only convinced her further that she was right.

"Fine. Play dumb. But thanks. I can't exactly say they're beautiful, but they will look perfect with my necklace. I'll think of you every time I wear them." She said the words without thinking, then realized her mistake. She didn't want to encourage him to think she'd be thinking of him. . . .

All that thinking was hurting her head.

"Hey, if you're thanking me, then maybe you think I did something worth being thanked for and would like to reciprocate by having dinner with me."

"TC, we talked about this . . ."

"As platonic friends," he insisted. "Nothing more."

"Nothing more?" She wasn't sure she believed him.

"Scouts' honor."

She laughed. He'd made the sign for her before. She could see him doing it now, squeezing those fingers together at his brow. "You were never a Boy Scout, were you?"

He didn't answer. Instead, he asked, "So, you'll come? Dinner at my house at six. I'll cook."

"As long as you understand that it's just a friendly meal and don't read anything more into it."

"Scouts' honor."

She snorted as she disconnected.

Eve was sure of a couple things.

That TC had left the earrings.

That he'd never been a Boy Scout.

And that, suddenly, her day looked brighter. And though she was sure her day was brighter, she wasn't exactly sure why.

"Nana Vancy, hurry up. I told her six, and she's not supposed to know you're helping me."

"She won't know. I will sneak out the back if I have to. I just want to be sure the dinner is perfect."

TC eyed the pot of chili on his stove that Nana Vancy was stirring. "I thought Hungarian food was your specialty."

"It is. But I'm sure your Eve would suspect it if that's what you served. Chili is much safer." She tapped the spoon on the pot and set it on the spoon rest. "So, tell me again, did she like the gift?"

"I think so. She told me they weren't beautiful— and they weren't. Neither is her necklace, though."

"But she told you that she'd think of you when she wore them?"

"Yes."

Nana Vancy pulled a cast-iron pan with cornbread in it out of the oven. "Perfect, if I do say so myself." She looked up at him. "And things between the two of you will be perfect as well. You'll feed her and maybe ask if she'll go with you and Bert on a walk."

"You want me to walk the dog with Eve?"

"It will be dark. The sky is clear, and there's a full moon. What could be more romantic? And when you get back, you'll both be cold, so you'll offer to warm her. . . ." Nana reached into her pocket and pulled out a sprig of mistletoe. "Put this in the entryway."

"She's going to be suspicious after the mistletoe minefield you created in the office."

"You tell her that my brilliant office decor was your inspiration."

Everything Nana Vancy had planned sounded plausible, as if it could work.

Should work, even.

But TC felt a small niggle of fear that something would go wrong. From what he'd gathered, Nana Vancy's plans habitually went awry.

Bert barked.

"Oh, that must be Eve," Nana said. "You go out to the front and get her. I'll sneak out the back."

She glanced at the mistletoe still in her hand and thrust it at him. "I really feel the mistletoe is important."

"Don't worry about it. I'm sure I can figure something out."

"Good luck." She gave a tug on his shirtsleeve, and TC leaned down obligingly and let her kiss his cheek. "You're a good boy," she assured him, then scurried out the kitchen door.

TC hurried to the front door. Bert was still barking like mad as he opened it. "I'm glad you came."

Eve came inside and didn't seem the least bit bothered by Bert's less than gentlemanly behavior. He jumped and continued his excited barking, and Eve bent down and rubbed his ears.

"Hey, Bert, behave," TC scolded.

"That's okay. Bert and I understand each other." She gave the dog one last pat on the head, then straightened and took off her coat.

TC wondered if he should offer to help her and almost did, but he worried she'd take offense. Some women did. Some women expected it. A guy never knew where he stood.

"Something smells great." Eve hung up her coat on the coat tree, then turned, looking at him.

"Oh. Oh, sorry. Come in. I hope you like chili."

"Love it."

"Great. Let's go into the kitchen. I thought about eating in the dining room, but I figured you'd be more comfortable and trust my intentions were pure if we ate casually in the kitchen."

She laughed. "You gave this some thought."

"I've discovered that you are a woman who requires thought, Eve."

"I'm as easygoing as they come," she argued.

"And that's what makes you so difficult. You think you're easygoing and low maintenance, but in truth, that makes you tougher. For instance, I was just hemming and hawing, trying to decide if you would take offense if I offered to help you off with your coat, or if you'd take offense that I didn't."

She laughed. "I didn't take offense that you didn't, but I wouldn't have if you did."

"Great. I can help with coats. How about doors?" he asked as he gestured to one of the stools at the counter.

Eve sat down and thought about his question a moment before responding. "If you're through the door first, you can hold it, but then, if I'm through the door first, you have to not mind if I hold it for you."

"Car doors? Do you expect a guy to go around and open yours?"

He stirred Nana's chili, hoping it lent an air of I-cooked-for-you ambience to the charade.

"A man walking around the car to open a woman's door always struck me as stupid. I can open a car door as well as a man can. Why should I sit there, twiddling my thumbs, waiting for him to walk around?"

"Great." He tapped the spoon and set it in the spoon rest. "Yes on coats, fifty-fifty on doors, and no on car doors. See? We're making progress."

"TC, we're not supposed to be 'making progress.' We're just friends, so this is all sort of moot."

He'd hoped she'd forgotten, but it was obvious she hadn't. "Fine. How about serving a friend dinner? Is that allowed?"

She laughed. "Yes, that is definitely allowed."

He brought the pan of cornbread to the island, got

out the butter, and then dished up two bowls of Nana's chili. "I'm having milk to drink. It's good to cool off spicy foods. You?"

"That's fine."

He brought over the milk and sat down on the stool next to hers. "Tell me what you think."

Eve dipped her spoon into the steaming, thick chili and blew on it for a second, then put it into her mouth. She smiled at him as she chewed.

Then her cheeks started to flush.

And her eyes started to water.

And suddenly she wasn't chewing, but instead screwed her eyes shut and swallowed. The action squeezed out more tears.

She opened her eyes, grabbed her glass of milk, and gulped it.

"Eve?"

She drained the glass of milk and shot him a rather forced smile. "Sorry. It was a bit spicier than I anticipated."

"It's that hot?" He took his own spoonful and put it into his mouth, and as the flames ripped through his sensitive tongue, he swallowed the bit pretty much whole and then gulped his own milk.

TC would have sworn in a court of law that he could feel the chili travel down his throat and land with a thud in his stomach. "Uh, yeah, it's that hot," he said, answering himself.

"Maybe if we simply dunked our cornbread in it?"

Eve cut a triangle of cornbread from the pan, put it on her plate, broke off a piece, then dropped it into her chili. "Could I have more milk, please? Just in case."

TC got up and poured them each another full glass, then watched as Eve gamely spooned up the bit of bread, now coated in chili, and put it into her mouth. She chewed, and though a faint flush rose again on her cheeks, there were no tears.

"Hey, that's pretty good. You try."

TC copied her actions and took his bite. This time, rather than a raging fire that threatened third-degree burns, there was simply a rush of heat that singed but didn't scorch. "You're right."

"That's the trick to the chili, I think. You have to use it as more of an accent than a main course."

"Or we could simply throw it out and I could have a pizza delivered."

"Where's your sense of adventure, TC? Life is much more interesting if you sometimes live on the wild side."

They continued with Eve's chili-eating method. The slight scorching in their mouths didn't really lend itself to in-depth conversation, but as they ate, TC noted that Eve was wearing the earrings.

"Do they match?" he asked.

She reached up and fingered one, then held up her necklace. "Very close."

"They don't get any prettier looking," he said with a grin.

"I learned a long time ago that there's more to pretty than surface appearances. The necklace has always represented Christmas to me, because—"

"Your parents gave it to you."

"Because they sacrificed to give it to me. It represents an unselfish sort of love."

"Like Santa Claus has."

She nodded and smiled. "Yes, like Santa Claus. Big gestures aren't necessary as far as I'm concerned. Things from the heart—those matter most. Those are what's pretty."

She pushed back slightly from the counter, putting a bit of distance between them. "So, why don't you let me help with the dishes?"

He laughed. "Sure. I'll add that to my list. Coats—okay. Doors—fifty-fifty. Car doors—never. Dishes—together."

They did the dishes.

It was a little thing, but it seemed sort of intimate, and Eve wasn't sure why. The whole evening seemed intimate, and there was no real reason it should. A bowl of lava masquerading as chili didn't make for true intimacy. But TC's growing list of her likes and dislikes did.

She finished washing the pan, and TC dried it and put it away. "Would you like to take a walk with us?"

At the word *walk,* Bert went from sleeping on the kitchen rug to wide awake and bounding in a split second.

"I really should be heading home. I have work tomorrow."

"Just a short walk?"

Bert jumped on her, as if he knew she held the fate of his walk in her hands. She laughed. "Sure. A quick one."

They both bundled up, and TC slipped Bert's lead on. He opened the door and held it as Eve walked out. She laughed as he assured her, "Next time you can get it for me."

She stood on the porch and waited as he locked the door. It was totally dark out, but there was a full moon shining on the pristine snow that blanketed TC's yard. "It's beautiful out here tonight."

"Yes, it is," TC said, standing right in front of her, Bert's lead in one hand, his free hand reaching out and gently grasping her at the waist. He pulled her gently toward him and said, "Look up."

She obliged and saw a sprig of mistletoe overhead.

"Nana?" she asked.

"Nana," he assured her. "Where do you stand on mistletoe? Does the guy get to kiss you under it, or do you kiss him?"

She should tell him that neither of his answers was an option. She was just out of a bad relationship, and she didn't need a rebound guy. Especially one who'd stood her up in the past. But even as she had the thought, she remembered TC's explanation for that and felt a jolt of sympathy.

He stood there, waiting, every bit the gentleman. Waiting for her to make up her mind.

She didn't. She couldn't.

Eve simply acted on instinct and leaned forward and kissed him.

This kiss was as hot as the chili and possibly just as dangerous for her, because she wasn't sure a milk chaser would work as a salve. She did not want to fall for another man.

Especially a man who could have his pick of women.

He was one of America's Most Eligible Bachelors, and she was just Eve Elisabeth Allen.

She broke off the kiss and said, "I really need to go home."

She sped down the stairs and to her car, calling, "Thanks for dinner!" over her shoulder.

As she backed out of the driveway and onto the street, she looked at TC standing on the porch, one gloved hand on his lips, the other hand holding Bert's leash.

She threw the car into gear and sped down the street. As she passed the Salos', it looked as if someone was standing in the doorway.

She didn't have to wonder who it was. She merely hoped that Nana Vancy hadn't seen her kiss TC.

Chapter Eight

". . . Two Turtledoves . . ."

It had been a long night. A very long night.

Thoughts of TC had kept playing through Eve's mind. Not that she'd dreamed of him.

No. Not one dream.

After all, she'd have to have slept in order to dream of him.

She pulled into Salo Construction's parking lot, thankful that this week she'd be the only one in.

No Noah.

No Mr. Salo.

And please, no Nana Vancy.

Even she didn't need to be here. But she'd asked Noah if he'd mind. She wanted to get the office totally reorganized and ready for the new year. He'd said no, he didn't mind, as long as she took some time off for the holiday.

"Bah, humbug," she muttered to herself.

She hadn't felt this anti-Christmas since the ninth grade. But even as she had that thought, she reached up and fingered the ugly earrings and felt a small niggle of jingle-bell-edness.

Just the tiniest fa-la-la and hall-decking shot of glee.

But she ruthlessly squashed the feelings down.

She had plans for this holiday. She was going to organize an office and forget about Christmas.

She opened the office door and flipped on the light.

There was something on her desk.

It wasn't wrapped.

It was a box of chocolate turtles from Pulakos and a bag of Dove chocolates. Underneath was an envelope.

She opened it and found a Christmas card that consisted of a picture of Bert wearing a Santa hat. Inside was a note. *Two boxes of turtles and Doves . . . two turtledoves. Get it? TC.*

She looked at the candy and started to laugh.

She picked up the phone and dialed his number.

She seemed to be calling him a lot lately. At this rate she was going to have to add his number to her speed-dial.

"Merry Christmas," TC answered.

"Thank you. You're nuts. And while I'll admit you

made me laugh, I'm going to beg you not to leave me any French hens tomorrow. Really, my neighbors wouldn't be impressed with a chicken coop in the backyard."

"Well, rats. There goes that idea," he teased.

And in her mind's eye she could see the crinkling at the corners of his eyes.

His slightly up-to-no-good smile.

She shook her head. She had to stop thinking about TC Potter. "Listen, I've got to get to work. I just wanted to say thank you. But really, TC, it's enough. We both know you have a lot of options for dates. You don't need me."

"I won't bother you again today." He should have sounded resigned. Annoyed, even. Instead, he sounded almost jovial, and that was dangerous.

"Well, all right then. Thanks and good-bye."

"Bye, Eve."

Yes, he sounded altogether too pleased with himself for Eve's liking.

She tried to decide what to do first in the office, but all she could do was stare at the candy.

It was only nine o'clock—far too early for chocolates.

But then, her good friend Deanne frequently told her that chocolate was a valid food group.

Of course, this was the same Deanne who considered taco joints five-star dining.

Still, one chocolate couldn't hurt, right?

She popped a turtle into her mouth and closed her eyes.

The chocolate was very good.

Being charmed by TC Potter?

Not so much.

Chapter Nine

". . . Three French Hens . . ."

"T c."

Eve was all smiles as she answered the door the following evening.

TC hoped that meant she'd missed him.

She looked pointedly at the basket in his right hand and said, "Please tell me you don't have hens in there."

"Hey, you warned me that your neighbors wouldn't like a coop in your backyard. And I could sort of see their point, although I would point out that Bert would love neighborhood chickens."

"So, what's in the basket?" she asked.

"If you invite me in, I'll show you."

"I thought we agreed yesterday that you were done with . . . well, whatever it is you're doing." She let him into the house.

TC set down the basket and took off his snow gear. "I love Erie, but I wish our winters were just a little shorter."

"This one has barely started," she pointed out.

Totally de-booted and de-coated, TC picked up the basket and started into her kitchen. He heard her sigh and follow.

He set the basket on the counter and said, "I didn't bring plates and silverware. Do you think you could supply those?"

"TC, I thought we agreed—" she started again.

He interrupted. "No, we never agreed. I said I wouldn't bother you again yesterday . . . and I didn't. And as long as we're talking about yesterday, I should probably set the record straight. You said I had options for dates, but you're wrong."

"No, I'm quite right. I know you've been chased by all kinds of women since last's year's most-eligible-bachelor article."

"Well, yes, there's that, but you misunderstood. Yes, there are women who would probably go out with me if I asked, but I haven't asked and don't intend to. I've met a woman who captivates me."

Eve snorted.

"Shh. I'm telling you about this woman I met. She's very efficient at work, but what really strikes me about her is her kindness. She indulges an older woman who comes up with crazy, albeit good-hearted schemes, and she is wonderful with kids. She looks at a beautiful winter's night with awe and wonder. She doesn't mind dog drool. She . . ." He let the sentence trail off, reached over, caught Eve's hand, and pulled her into a kiss. It wasn't nearly as intimate as he'd have liked—it was more of a quick buss than anything—but he didn't want her to kick him out before they'd eaten, and he knew that even a light kiss was pushing her.

"And all those are reasons enough to want to date her, but there's something more. This woman is kind and has this capacity to forgive that I admire. She touches me in ways I don't understand. I've met a lot of women this last year, but I didn't feel connected to any of them. But this woman I've only just met, and . . ." He shrugged. "There's no way to describe how she makes me feel centered when I'm with her and how I feel adrift when I'm not."

Eve was just standing there, not responding, simply standing where he'd left her after he kissed her. He figured he'd said enough for one night. "So, how about those plates, some silverware, and wineglasses if you have them?"

As if awakening from a fog, Eve went and gathered place settings and came back to the island.

He took them. "So, are you going to ask what's in the basket?"

Asking what was in the basket was a much easier question than all the others that were rattling around in Eve's mind. "What's in the basket, TC?"

He opened the lid with a flourish. "Since you didn't want French hens in a coop in the backyard, I went with Cornish hens and a loaf of French bread, which I thought came close."

"As close as turtles and Doves."

He laughed. "I think I get to take a few liberties. I mean, really, what woman wants real partridges or hens of any kind?"

"The song does seem to be a bit bird heavy. Maybe back when it was written, birds were all the rage?"

It was inane chatter at best, but inane was so much better than TC's list of reasons he was pursuing her. She really didn't want to think about what he'd said. She didn't want to sort out her very confused feelings. She just wanted to sit down and enjoy a meal with TC. In order to do that, the more inane the better.

He pulled out an insulated bag, opened it, and took out two Cornish hens, then another insulated bag with pilaf in it. Lastly, he pulled out a bottle of wine. "It's a Riesling from Ferrente's."

"I don't know that one," she said, pointing to the label. Erie County was known for its wineries.

"It's a winery just over the border in Ohio. They've got a great restaurant. We'll go sometime."

Eve didn't comment on going sometime. That was not inane conversation. Instead she said, "You should have brought Bert. He's probably lonely alone at the house."

"Nah. I may go out from time to time to research

an article, but most days I'm at home with him, writing. I think he enjoys a bit of alone time. I'll get back tonight and probably find him sprawled out on the couch, which means I'll have to sit in a recliner, because once Bert claims a seat, there's no moving him. Once, I tried . . ."

And as easily at that, Eve had steered the conversation to safer ground. No more talking about what TC was up to, about any attraction.

Just a pleasant dinner, fun stories, and his company.

And after dinner, as they sat on the couch watching *It's a Wonderful Life,* Eve realized that TC's company was definitely the highlight of a very nice evening, and she wasn't sure what to do with that realization.

"You're sure you don't mind the movie?" she asked for the umpteenth time. "It's been my experience that men prefer explosions and car chases to angels and tinkling bells."

"There you go, generalizing again, Eve. Men watch *It's a Wonderful Life.* Sometimes we even get a bit teary. But, being men, we try to hide it."

"Why? Own your tears, I say," she teased.

"Because for all our bravado, men worry about letting too much emotion show. If we did, then women might discover how easily wounded we actually are. And we—men as a species—wouldn't like that at all."

She laughed. "I swear, I won't tell the rest of the female species if you tear up," she said.

"Good." He nonchalantly placed an arm around her shoulders.

Eve's first instinct was to pull away, but she stopped herself. His arm over her shoulders felt rather right. Comforting. Anchoring.

So, instead of pulling away, she leaned into him and concentrated on the movie. A movie where she knew the ending would be a happy one.

That was the great thing about classics. You knew you were going to get that happily-ever-after.

A woman could count on it.

Believe in it.

In real life, it was much harder to believe.

When the movie ended to the sound of a tinkling bell, TC stood and said, "I should probably go and let you get some sleep. You have work tomorrow." He started to gather up his things. That accomplished, he walked to the door.

Eve trailed after him, not sure what to say.

TC put his coat and boots back on, and before he picked up the basket, he kissed her lightly on the cheek. "See you tomorrow."

"TC, you really don't have to—"

He laughed. "I know I don't have to. I want to. And if you don't mind, I'd like to pick you up around three from work."

"Please, swear to me you won't buy me any birds, calling or otherwise."

He held up a hand, two fingers at his brow. "Scout's honor."

"You were never a Boy Scout," she said, not for the first time.

He ignored her comment and repeated, "Tomorrow at three? I know the office is closed, and you're writing your own schedule, so that shouldn't be a problem, right?"

Eve didn't need to ask where he got his information. He had a Nana Vancy connection that probably got him any info he wanted. "Fine. Three."

"Don't sound so excited," he scolded as he cheerily picked up the basket.

"That wasn't excitement. That was trepidation."

He was laughing as he opened the door and headed out to his truck.

Eve stood in the entryway, watching through the window as he backed out and disappeared down the street.

What was she going to do about TC Potter?

Before she could figure out the answer to that question, she had to figure out, how did she feel about him?

Yes, that was the big question.

How did she feel about her ex-Christmas nemesis?

Eve didn't have a clue.

Chapter Ten

". . . Four Calling Birds . . ."

The next day, TC arrived promptly at three.

Eve was just finishing putting the last files back when he walked in the door. She smiled wondering what he had up his sleeve for today.

"Are you ready?" he asked.

She nodded. "I just finished. Salo Construction is now completely organized. I still want to implement a couple of computer systems, but for now I'm pleased. The closet is once again for coats, not for storing overflow files."

"Good for you."

"Thanks." And she realized that having someone to share her accomplishment with made getting the job done all that much sweeter. "Thanks for listening."

"I like listening to you."

She didn't know what to say to that. All the possibilities she could think of sounded way too over the top in her head, so she settled for saying, "Ditto."

"Come on, then, let's get going."

"Please tell me that if I get into your truck, I won't find it stuffed with birds."

"Hey, the song says four calling birds, and that would never stuff my truck. It's a big truck—a manly truck, after all." She must have looked a bit nervous, because he laughed and said, "But, no. There are no birds, stuffed or otherwise, in my truck."

"Okay, then." She quickly bundled up and followed TC to his un-birded truck.

"So, where are we going?" she asked when they got on the road.

"Well, you're right—today is four-calling-birds day—but since you made your feelings clear on that, I came up with an alternate plan."

She noticed he didn't say what the plan was. But rather than asking that question, she asked, "Do you plan to keep this up for all twelve days? Because really, TC, it's not necessary."

"Listen, I've ruined two of your Christmases. Anything I can do to brighten this one is only right. And this *is* brightening it, right?"

For the first time since they'd remet, TC sounded uncertain.

"Yes, your surprises are definitely brightening it. You know, I encouraged my parents to go on their trip over the holidays. I thought it would be great—no pretending to be all holiday spirit-y when I was feeling anything but—but now I'm regretting it. They won't be back until January, and I've realized I'm going to miss them. Then you came along and . . . well, I still miss them, but not as much."

"I'm glad. I owed you a nice holiday."

Suddenly she wondered if that's what this was. Some strange attempt to make up for his Christmases past.

But giving her the twelve days of Christmas was one thing—well, actually, twelve things—but kissing her? That was another thing entirely.

She might not know TC well, but she didn't think he was the kind of man who'd kiss her without having some feeling behind it.

She could ask him to define just what that feeling was, but she wasn't sure she wanted to know. Because if he defined his feelings, she might have to try to define hers, and she wasn't sure she could.

And even if she could, she wasn't sure she was ready to.

So she didn't ask. She didn't say anything else as the truck went over Thirty-eighth Street. But when TC turned the corner and pulled into the Erie Zoo's parking lot, she said, "The zoo? Isn't it closed for the winter?"

"One of my friends who works here offered to give us a private tour. Since you didn't want me to bring you any birds, I thought we could go visit four here, if that's okay."

Eve started laughing. "Four calling birds at the zoo is just about perfect, TC."

She followed him to the gate and was surprised to realize that it wasn't only the zoo that was just about perfect . . . it was TC as well.

The question was, what did she want to do about it?

TC's friend took them down into the basement of the main building, where a lot of the animals who couldn't winter outside were kept. Later Eve and TC walked through the outdoor part of the zoo and admired the animals that did winter outside. They were standing in front of the polar bears when Eve realized TC had taken her hand.

She wasn't sure when he'd done it, and she couldn't figure out why that was.

Finally it hit her.

She hadn't noticed that he was holding her hand because it felt so right.

And, as if on cue, it started to snow.

Standing in front of the two polar bears in the snow, holding TC's hand . . . it felt right.

And the fact that it did scared Eve.

She'd hardly just remet TC.

It was too soon.

And it was way too soon after her breakup.

She'd promised herself a man hiatus.

And she was pretty sure this wasn't it.

But when TC gave the hand he was holding a little tug and pulled her toward him, Eve didn't just wait for a kiss. She kissed him first.

Even though she knew she was breaking her own rule.

But as she kissed TC, she simply didn't care.

Because if holding his hand had felt right, this felt even righter.

She was sure the thought would scare her later, but for right now she simply relished it.

Chapter Eleven

". . . Five Golden Rings . . ."

The next morning, Eve awoke with a start and realized that today, on the TC Christmas count, was day five. And five wasn't a bird.

She hurried out to her purse for her cell, which was where she had saved TC's phone number. It wasn't in the left pocket, where she always kept it. She felt a spurt of panic.

She'd lost her cell phone.

Eve had read horror stories about people who lost theirs, only to have someone find them and run up huge charges.

Eve never lost anything.

Never.

She lived her life according to a certain organizational code that didn't allow for losing things.

She opened her purse and looked inside, even as she got ready to look up her carrier's contact number. Then, as a last resort, she checked the right pocket of her purse and found the cell.

Her nerves immediately calmed down. There would be no thousand-dollar cell-phone bill.

All was well.

When her elation died down, she remembered why she'd been looking for her phone and hurriedly called TC.

"Hello?" he said groggily.

"Did I wake you?" she asked, feeling a bit guilty. She hadn't realized how early it was.

"No. Bert did that about five minutes ago. But I wish you had. Waking up to you would be so much nicer than waking up to him."

She wasn't sure what to say to that, and her silence must have stretched on a bit too long, because TC said, "Did you need something, or did you just call to say that you miss me?"

"No. I called to tell you no golden rings. A pair of earrings, birds at the zoo, some chocolates, and cornish hens for dinner are one thing—"

He interrupted her. "Actually, they're four things."

Eve laughed, but it sounded tinny and nervous to her own ears. "Fine, they're four things, not one. But I wanted to be absolutely clear . . . don't buy me any gold."

"Hey, I know it's too early in our relationship for that."

Relationship? The word had her panicking more than the thought of losing her cell phone had. More than worrying about golden rings had. "We don't have a relationship."

He laughed. "Yes, we do. Nana Vancy's sure she's got some mystical Hungarian sixth sense, and she assures me that we do indeed have a relationship. And I'm not going to argue with her. *Or* with you, for that matter. At least not right now. I've got to go. My coffee's almost ready, and I'll be more human after a cup."

"No gold," she insisted, but she was talking to air.

He'd hung up on her.

He'd insisted they had a relationship.

And he hadn't promised no gold.

She wasn't sure which was more annoying. All three things were annoying, she told herself, but she suspected she wasn't listening, because she found herself smiling.

There was something about TC. She wasn't sure what it was, but she was pretty sure she didn't want to find out. Maybe he'd take her warning to heart and leave her be today.

As if on cue, her cell phone rang.

But it wasn't her generic ring, which sounded like any normal land line ring. It was a ring tone—a song she recognized as Eva Cassidy's "Fields of Gold."

Eve stared at the phone as it continued playing the clip over and over. She loved that song, but she knew she hadn't programmed that ring tone into her phone.

Oh, no. What if she really had lost her phone and picked up someone else's? Another phone that looked like hers? If she had lost hers, it had to have been at the zoo yesterday. But she didn't remember having her cell out at the zoo.

The ring tone started playing another cycle, and she realized she'd better pick up. She flipped the phone open and said "Hello?" hesitantly.

"Hey, Eve, it's me again." Before she could respond, TC—the 'me' in question—said, "Oops. Gotta go. I'll call you right back."

Well, that answered that. It was her phone. She hadn't picked up someone else's by accident.

But then how had she gone from a nice, normal ring to the musical ring tone?

She flipped her phone open and started to go into the menu when the phone rang again, playing the same ring tone. Beyond frustrated, she flipped it open.

"I just wanted to say . . ." A crackling noise roared her in ear, and she realized she'd lost the connection.

She snapped the phone shut and waited.

For a third time it rang, and once again Eva Cassidy crooned about golden fields until Eve flipped the phone open. "TC, what is going on?"

"I wanted to tell you that I am not buying you a golden ring, much less five golden rings. It's way too early in our relationship for that."

"I'm relieved." Relieved, confused, annoyed . . . and maybe a bit amused. She wasn't sure what TC was up to, but he sounded so pleased with himself.

"But I'm not ruling out—" More crackling noises.

It didn't sound like ordinary static.

As a matter of fact, it sounded like someone making a gurgling noise in the back of his throat.

"TC?"

There was a click, then silence, as if TC had hung up.

Again the ring tone. But this time poor Eva's voice hardly got past saying she never took promises lightly when Eve snapped the phone open.

"TC, I know you well enough by now to realize you're up to something. I'm just not sure what."

"Do you think these last couple of weeks have let you get to know me pretty well?" he asked.

"Yes. And I—"

"So, does that mean you acknowledge that I know you pretty well too?"

"That's not what this is about, although I really don't know *what* this is about—"

There was more crackling and then the sound of TC's laughter before the connection was broken again.

Eve shut the phone and waited for Eva's first note; then she snapped the phone open. "TC."

"There. That's five 'golden' rings." He laughed so hard, he couldn't say anything else.

Finally it all made sense. Why her cell phone had mysteriously jumped pockets. Why it had gone from a nice, normal ring to a ring tone. " 'Fields of Gold.' A ring tone. Five calls." Eve shook her head. "You're insane, Potter."

"Insane about you," he said. "And I might point out that you all but admitted you're insane about me too."

"I did not. I simply admitted I was getting to know you, and what I know is, you're nuts."

"Yeah, but you like it. Even if you don't want to, you do. You like that I'm insane, and you like me. That's a lot for one day."

"I'm not admitting to anything," she said. Though to herself she could maybe admit that there was some truth to what he was saying. Her heart tended to do this weird little leap every time he was around, and when he wasn't around, all she could do was think about him and when he'd be around next, so maybe . . .

"See you tomorrow, Eve." This time he didn't make fake crackling noises. He just hung up.

Eve stared at her cell phone for a minute.

She had no clue what she was going to do about TC Potter.

Chapter Twelve

". . . Six Geese a-Laying . . ."

Eve woke up with a sense of anticipation.

Six geese?

What on earth could TC have planned?

She was pretty sure she'd covered the no-live-birds rule and hoped that, whatever he did, he took her rule to heart and didn't involve real geese. She could only imagine the mess they'd make. No. She absolutely wasn't taking possession of any geese today, no matter how much TC . . .

She paused and tried to think of the right word.

Annoyed?

Maybe at one time but not anymore.

She fingered her earrings. She'd worn them every day since he gave them to her.

Intrigued?

Well, yes, that was a good description. The way TC's mind worked was certainly intriguing. But she felt something more than that.

She felt . . .

Happy.

Plain and simple, TC made her happy. It didn't matter if he was annoying her, teasing her, intriguing her, or just sharing a moment with her. He made her happy.

She half waited for a phone call or the doorbell as she got ready for her day, but the house remained strangely silent. She had hoped she'd spend the day with TC, but since he hadn't called or showed up, she wasn't sure.

Rather than waiting around, she could go into the office. She might have finished setting up the new filing system—which really amounted to setting up a filing system, because the Salos didn't seem to have any system at all with their filing attempts.

But even though the filing was systemized now, there were a couple of other jobs she could do. One of the worst ones involved the small kitchen at the back of the building. There were things in that cupboard that were covered in dust, and Eve was pretty sure that any food around long enough to gather dust was too old for human consumption.

Yes. Tackling the kitchen was a great way to see

that she didn't sit at home waiting for TC's next insane act. Yet, as she worked in the quiet office kitchen, she waited.

Every time there was the sound of traffic on the road, she hurried to the window.

Twice the office phone rang.

Both were business calls from people who didn't realize Salo's had shut down for a holiday break.

Lunchtime was especially trying. She took a couple of obligatory bites of her sandwich but found she wasn't very hungry.

By the time she drove home at three, the kitchen at the Salo office was sparkling, and she had a list of items she planned to pick up.

She also had this let-down feeling she couldn't shake as she drove through the snow-covered streets.

The main routes weren't too bad, but the side streets were in rough shape. She wondered if she'd have to shovel out her driveway in order to get the car in, but as she approached it, she saw that it was fairly clear, probably only an inch of snow covering it.

That was strange, because more than two inches of snow had fallen over the course of the day.

Not only was there not quite enough snow covering the drive, but something else was amiss. Rather than feeling nervous, Eve felt a jolt of excitement.

TC hadn't forgotten.

She turned off the car and looked at her lawn.

There were snow-covered lumps near the sidewalk to the porch.

She hurried to one and brushed the snow off.

It was a lawn goose.

A goose wearing a red winter cape and bonnet.

She brushed off the next one and found a second goose, this one wearing a tartan plaid cape.

She continued brushing until she'd exposed six geese, all wearing holiday capes.

Laughing, she let herself into the house, kicked off her boots, and hit TC's speed-dial number before she even started taking off her coat.

"Hello, Eve. How was your day?" he asked, his voice the picture of innocence.

Eve knew she should try for restraint, but she couldn't quite manage. "Oh, TC, I love them."

"Ah, you found your geese, huh? I wondered if you'd be home and I'd have to try to sneak them into place with you inside. But you weren't."

She didn't admit that she'd left because she didn't want to sit home waiting for him. She'd done that with Pat the Rat—contentedly waited for him whenever he got busy.

Until the one night she got tired of waiting and went to Naomi's for company and saw his car.

And as she peeked in the window, she'd seen the two of them.

No, she was through waiting around for men.

But even if she hadn't waited, she was glad TC had shown up.

"I was afraid you'd forget the rules and send real geese. Those would have been very messy."

"I know better than to send you something messy. You like order."

"What else do you know about me?" she asked before she could censor herself and stop the words.

"More than you think I know," came his cryptic response.

"Did you know I was calling not only to thank you but also to invite you to dinner?"

There was a long pause. "Now, that I didn't know."

She laughed. "I may surprise you yet. So, are you too busy?"

"I'm putting my boots on even as we speak."

She laughed, and again it struck her that when TC was around, even if it was only on the phone, she spent a lot of time laughing.

"Great. Guess I'd better get cooking then."

"I'll be there in fifteen minutes . . . or less."

Eve hung up the phone and couldn't help but wonder where her invitation had come from. She hadn't intended to issue it.

But as she thought about it, she realized she was glad she had.

Now, what on earth to make for a man who'd just given her six lawn geese?

She discovered there was nothing—absolutely

nothing—that could be prepared in short order in her kitchen. She'd planned on making herself a sandwich, but she couldn't feed a sandwich to a man who'd given her six geese.

She thought about making reservations, but to be honest—at least with herself—she didn't want to share TC with a crowd tonight. She wanted him to herself. She wanted to talk to him, to share her day with him, and have him share his day with her.

She wanted to sit on the couch and watch something—anything—on television, or a movie, or read books next to each other. She just wanted to spend time with TC.

So she did the next best thing. She called and ordered in Chinese.

And she was waiting a few minutes later when he showed up at her door with Bert. "You mentioned him the other night," he said by way of greeting as she opened the door. "So I hope you don't mind."

"Hey, Bert," she said, and she knelt next to the dog.

"I hope you don't mind, but after I made the invitation, I realized I didn't have anything to serve you, so I ordered in Chinese from the Fortune Garden."

"Eve, I'll confess, I didn't hurry over here for the food. You could have served me cheese and crackers, and I'd have been happy."

"Oh."

"Aren't you going to ask why I did hurry over?"

She sensed that that was a dangerous question, one

she wasn't quite ready to hear the answer to, but that didn't stop her from asking, "Why did you hurry over?"

"Because I missed you. I missed this." And he kissed her. There was no mistletoe to blame, no Nana Vancy machinations.

There was just her.

And TC.

And Bert, lounging at their feet.

And a kiss that was tender and sweet . . . everything a kiss should be.

All Eve's rules and reservations flew out the window with that kiss. She could stay like this, in his arms, forever.

But eventually the real world intervened, and the doorbell rang. Eve pulled back and sounded breathless to her own ears as she said, "I bet that's our dinner."

TC asked, "Would we break your rules if I asked to pay?"

"Yes. I invited you, so I pay."

He nodded. "And next time I invite you out, I pay? No more having to go dutch? It will be a real date?"

She ignored him as she opened the door, took the bag, and handed the delivery boy the money. "Thanks."

Then, dinner in hand, she turned back to TC. "Yes. Next time you ask me out, I won't pay my half. You can pay for the whole thing. A date. A real date."

He grinned. "Well, then, that's fine. Yes on coats.

Fifty-fifty on doors. No on car doors. And whoever invites can pay on *dates*." He put a heavy emphasis on the word *dates*.

Eve waited for her nerves to spike. But they didn't. So she simply held up the bag and said, "Let's eat."

TC knew he was making progress with Eve. She'd barely blinked when he'd used the word *date*. They'd had a lovely dinner on her coffee table as they watched the evening news together, then sat back to watch a sitcom. Bert nosed his way in between them and plopped his head on Eve's lap. She didn't complain when the dog started to snore, and TC could only imagine how damp her jeans were getting from the dog drool. But still no complaint.

And when he put his arm over her shoulders, she didn't pull away. She snuggled closer.

TC enjoyed the sensation of just relaxing with Eve.

He'd gone on dates before, but none of them was exactly comfortable. The women wanted real dates: fancy restaurants, dancing, parties. They all wanted excitement, action.

Eve was content just to be with him and Bert.

And TC was equally content to be with her.

He could imagine doing this for years to come. Coming home to Eve and Bert.

Making dinner together.

Hanging out and reading or watching a show.

He could imagine the occasional dinner at the Salos.

Yes, as he looked at his future, he discovered what he couldn't imagine was not having Eve in it.

He felt something more for Eve than he'd ever felt for anyone. He wasn't quite ready to name it, but it was there and growing.

He didn't want to play any more games. He wanted this . . . her. He wanted her in his life. Nana Vancy was going to be thrilled.

And suddenly TC realized how he wanted to end his Twelve Days of Christmas. There was a lot to do, and he'd better get started. "Listen, Eve, this Twelve Days of Christmas was fun, but I don't want you to be disappointed tomorrow when there are no swans. Because, really, I think you've had enough birds, and I had to end it somewhere. I'm pretty sure I'd be hard-pressed to find maids, ladies, lords, pipers, and drummers too."

She laughed. "TC, that's not a problem. The last six days, you've been so creative. I've had fun, and I appreciate it."

"So, have I obliterated those memories of Christmases past when I ruined your holiday?" he asked, kissing her forehead gently.

Eve nodded. "More than made up for it, and to be honest, you didn't need to."

"I did. But even if the 'twelve days' business is over, there're still a few days before Christmas. I'd like to spend them with you."

Eve didn't answer immediately. She paused as if thinking, and TC found he was holding his breath.

"TC, I can think of a hundred reasons to say no. . . ."

"Name two," he demanded.

"Huh?"

"I bet you can't name a hundred, and I won't insist you try. Name just two."

She frowned, as if concentrating. "I recently broke up with someone."

"That's not a reason to say no. It means you're free and clear—no having to win you away from another man."

"You'd be my rebound guy," she pointed out.

"Do you play basketball?"

"Not well. I was quite unathletic."

"But you know the game a bit, so you understand that when a ball rebounds to you, sometimes you pass it off to a teammate, but sometimes you take it to the hoop yourself. Maybe I'm going for the hoop. Rebound, recent breakup—no valid excuse yet."

She didn't try to come up with another. "I was going to say that, although I could think of a hundred reasons not to see you, there's one good reason to keep seeing you. I'd miss you if I didn't. But while I'll admit that, I'm still nervous about wanting . . . and maybe learning to need . . . you. I'm uncertain, but you? You seem sure of yourself. Why?"

"Well, there's this Hungarian grandmother who had a feeling about us—and there's the fact that you kissed me. You can't lie when you kiss someone. I know you like me. And I like you. You even like my dog. We're both free and clear. . . ." He moved a bit closer with each word, and by the time he got to *clear,* he was right in front of her. As close as he could be without actually touching her.

Without pulling her toward him, he simply leaned in and kissed her.

She had every opportunity to back away.

And yet she didn't.

She met his kiss.

And when they finally broke apart, TC whispered, "Kisses don't lie. Say you'll go out with me tomorrow. Spend the day with me."

She laughed. "Yes. But you don't need to bring me swans or ladies or lords. Just bring me you and maybe Bert."

Chapter Thirteen

"What Are You Doing New Year's Eve?"

"**Y**ou can't stop now," Nana Vancy said, her voice filled with annoyance.

TC had been getting ready to leave when Nana Vancy appeared at his door. He was going to drive to Niagara Falls with Eve. The two-hour drive would provide a lot of time in the car for talking, and the Falls themselves were romantic. Even in the winter they were romantic.

And he wasn't going to admit it to Nana, but romantic with Eve was appealing. "Nana, she said I didn't need to bring her any more things."

It was Saturday. Christmas was the following Friday. TC was toying with the idea of a charm bracelet with all the song's items on it, but he wasn't going to bring swans or lords or any of the rest to Eve. "Nana,

I don't think I need a crutch like that in order to woo her. At least not anymore."

Nana smiled a knowing smile. "So you're wooing her openly now?"

"Yes."

"And I was the one who set you up, right?" It didn't take any type of insight to see that Nana Vancy was gloating. Gloating a lot. "I mean, I knew before either of you did that you and Eve were meant to be together."

TC sighed. If he answered honestly, there was a good chance that she'd never stop. But then again, if everyone she set up was as happy as TC currently was, then all was well. So with mental apologies to all her future, potentially unwilling matches, he found himself grinning as he said, "Yes, Nana. You knew it first."

"Then listen to me now when I tell you that you need to finish the song. It was such a perfect idea—don't let it go. I have a feeling that things won't be settled with you and Eve until the song is finished."

"Nana . . ." He tried to infuse his tone with all the warning he could muster. "Really, I don't want to—"

"And you don't have to. Just leave it to me, and I'll take care of everything." And with that offer—or threat—his neighbor turned around and started back across the driveway to her house.

Fine. He'd just tell Eve it was out of his hands, and

she'd understand, he was sure. That's how Eve was. Understanding.

He left for Eve's then, even though he knew he was early. He could use Nana's possible return as an excuse, but the truth was, he just wanted to see Eve.

He was sure Eve would understand that too.

TC hurried up to the door and knocked, eager to start the day. Eve opened it a second later.

At first he was flattered that she'd be so eager, she was waiting for him, but then he saw someone else standing in her entryway.

Someone big.

Someone smiling.

Someone very male.

"Sorry, TC. I'm going to have to take a rain check for our trip today."

"Problem?" he asked, trying to ignore the large, lurking man.

"This is Pat, my ex-boss."

Her ex-boss and ex-boyfriend. The one who'd stolen her work and claimed it as his own and then cheated on her with her best friend.

The man extended his hand, but TC blatantly ignored it. "Again, is there a problem?" he asked.

Eve glanced back at the guy, then looked at TC and shook her head. "No. Not really. Pat just needs some help, and—"

"Pardon us a minute." TC took Eve's hand, led her

out onto the porch, and shut the door. "What are you thinking?"

"What?" Eve looked genuinely confused.

TC didn't understand how Eve could stand there looking at him as if she didn't get it. "That's the guy who stole your work before. The man who cheated on you with your best friend. Why would you do anything to help him now?"

"Because . . ." She shrugged. "I don't have a good answer for you, other than to say that he needs me and I feel sorry for him. Naomi dumped him, and he's in danger of losing his job."

"Good."

"No, not good. I can't be that way, TC. I know I should kick him out and let him sink, but I'm over him, and this is just an hour or two of my time. My treating him as poorly as he treated me doesn't even anything out. It won't make me feel better." She paused. "I know it took a great deal for him to come here and not only apologize but also ask for my help. That's something he's never done before. He's grown."

"So you're going to toss me aside in order to help your ex?" He felt a sense of panic. He'd talked so confidently about not being Eve's rebound guy, but what if that's exactly what he was? Or, worse, what if he was her filler guy—someone to hang with until her real-deal guy came back?

"TC, it's one day. We could go tomorrow or—"

"Never mind."

"You know, when you listed the things you liked about me, you said, 'Your kindness, your capacity to forgive.' But what you meant was, you liked those character traits only when they applied to you." She was angry.

That hadn't been his intent. He was the angry one. She should be chagrined. Apologetic, even. Not righteously angry. "Eve, that's not what I meant."

"Listen, I'll call you later."

"Eve . . ."

"Later, TC. I'll talk to you later." She turned and hurried back into the house, shutting the door in his face.

That had gone well.

TC walked back to his truck.

It was going to be a very long day.

Eve went back into the house and glared at Pat the Rat.

Okay, that was a mean thought.

But she didn't care. Pat was a rat.

"Who was that?" he asked, his tone demanding.

"I don't think you're here to learn about my relationships, so why don't we—"

"Relationship?" Pat frowned.

She ignored the question and his expression. This was business. That's all it was. "Okay, give me your laptop, and let me see if I can get this straightened out for you. While I do that, you just sit there quietly and stop asking personal questions that you have no right to ask."

"But I . . ."

He must have sensed she was serious, because he went into the living room, plopped down in his favorite chair, and sat silently.

Eve grabbed the laptop, set it up on the coffee table, and started sorting through the mess he'd made of her filing system there.

"How did you manage to destroy a spreadsheet?" she asked. Before he could answer, she added, "Never mind. Anything I say is rhetorical. Just be quiet."

She continued muttering to herself for the next two hours while she reorganized the information on his laptop.

Then she sat back on the couch, arched her spine, rolled her neck, and looked back at her ex.

He'd dozed off about forty-five minutes in, and she'd been happy to let him sleep. He was a lot less trouble that way.

She studied him as if seeing him for the first time. His very blond hair was thinning . . . a lot. And how had she never noticed how sallow his complexion was? With his head back against the chair, his skin sort of sagged.

He couldn't hold a candle to TC in looks.

Far more important, he couldn't hold a candle to TC in the way he made her feel. He'd been comfortable, convenient, even.

TC definitely didn't make her . . . comfortable. He was always touching her, kissing her, doing odd things like leaving geese in her yard. She never knew what he'd do next, and because Eve was someone who liked to know what to expect, that should have made her decidedly *un*comfortable. And on some level it did.

But she had to confess, she liked the way she felt with TC. Never knowing what he was going to do or what he was going to talk her into doing.

Pat awoke with a snort. "You finished?"

"Yes, it's all done. And that was the one and only time I'll do it for you, so you'll probably want to think about learning to take care of your files yourself or hiring a new assistant."

"I did hire someone. Naomi."

Eve frowned. Her ex-friend had her boyfriend and now her old job?

"She's not very good," he added.

"I thought she dumped you."

"She dumps me on a regular basis," he grumbled.

Eve waited to feel jealous. To feel that same sense of righteous indignation she'd felt when she'd first found out about Naomi and the rat.

Nothing.

She felt absolutely nothing except a sense of gratitude that he was no longer her problem. "Well, maybe you should hire someone based on abilities, not on looks." She stood. "But it's time for you to go. Don't come again."

Pat stubbornly remained seated. "Eve, this wasn't the only reason I came over today. It was an excuse to see you. After you left, I realized I'd made a huge mistake. I know you're probably all tied up with your parents for Christmas day, but I thought . . . Well, what are you doing New Year's Eve? The company's throwing this big bash, and I know everyone would like to see you."

"What about Naomi?" she asked.

"She's going home to Wisconsin for Christmas. She'd never know."

"So you want to cheat on her with me?" How had she never noticed what a dork he was?

"Not *cheat*," he assured her with a little smile. "Just go out for an evening. I've missed you, Eve."

Pathetic. This man she'd wasted a year and a half on was pathetic.

What did that make her?

"No, Pat the R— uh, never mind. I just need you to understand that if you were the last man on earth, and I was the last woman, the answer would still be no. Now, take your computer and leave."

"Why did you help me if you weren't interested? I mean, you even kicked your boyfriend out for me."

She started walking toward the door, intending to be clear about wanting him to leave.

She heard him following, and as she stood in front of the door, she answered his question. "Why did I help you? Because, before, you had the control. I worked for you. You ended our relationship when you stole my idea and cheated. This time, I'm in control. You needed me, I helped, and now I'm telling you to leave. Don't come back. Don't call. And though I don't owe her anything, and though she might not believe me, maybe I'll drop Naomi a line to let her know that, if for some strange reason she wants to keep you, she might need to rethink her Christmas trip to Wisconsin."

Pat the Rat frowned. "You've changed, Eve."

"Maybe. Once upon a time I was willing to wear blinders for you, but I'm seeing things more clearly now. And, clearly, you are a rat, Pat. I like things orderly. And while on the surface TC might seem chaotic because he does so many unpredictable things, there's something I hadn't realized. He's someone I can count on. And there's comfort in that."

Yes, she could count on TC. She loved that about him.

Loved that.

Loved him.

She loved TC Potter?

Eve mulled over the idea of loving TC. The idea should have been scary. They'd only known each other for such a short time. And yet . . .

She loved him.

But before she could tell him, she had to totally move beyond her past. That meant getting rid of the big dork in front of her.

Pat whispered her name. "Eve . . ."

"Good-bye." She practically pushed him out the door and then turned her mind to what she needed to do next.

She needed to see TC about some swans.

Chapter Fourteen

". . . Seven Swans a-Swimming . . ."

TC spent the day working on his mall Santa article. He'd had writer's block in the past, but today it had mutated from block to inability.

He couldn't seem to get a word onto the computer screen. And if he did manage to type something, he'd realize it was bad moments after the letters appeared on the screen.

He almost wished he composed on a typewriter. There would be something so very satisfying about ripping a piece of paper from the typewriter, balling it up, and shooting it at the wastebasket.

Instead, he used his cursor and highlighted sections, then hit Delete for the umpteenth time.

It was all Eve's fault.

He wasn't jealous. He'd never been a jealous man. But he wasn't happy.

What was she thinking, helping out her ex? The guy didn't deserve any help. He'd hurt Eve. What if he convinced her to give him another chance?

TC wanted to warn her.

He wanted to call and tell her to be careful, but he didn't.

He wanted to write, but he couldn't.

All in all, Eve Allen had totally messed up his day. What if she decided to take her ex back? If that happened, TC suspected that more than just his day would be ruined.

He liked Eve.

But today, as he sat at his desk not writing, he couldn't help but think there was a chance that he more than liked her.

He suspected there was a chance that he *much* more than liked her. He'd realized over a Chinese dinner that he could picture her in his future.

And now he realized he couldn't picture a future without her.

He wasn't ready to name the feeling. To say *the* word. The big word. But he suspected that the feeling in his chest didn't need a word to define it. It was there. It was big. And it was growing.

He looked at the screen. All he had written was "Ho-ho-ho!"

Did that qualify as a word?

He didn't think so. And this time TC didn't bother highlighting and hitting Delete. He simply admitted defeat and closed the file. When the computer asked if he wanted to save his work, he clicked No.

The unwritten page disappeared. Gone into oblivion.

He wished his worry could be turned off that easily.

Maybe he'd call Eve.

As if on cue, the doorbell rang.

TC hurried to the door and found . . . Nana Vancy on his porch, wrapped in a sturdy shawl and wearing boots. "I thought you were spending the day with Eve," she said as she walked into his hall. "What happened?"

"Eve had an unexpected conflict, and we didn't go." Oh, yeah, her ex was a conflict all right.

"Did you figure out a swan gift like I said? I've got an idea for the rest, but the swan—I can't think of anything."

"I haven't been thinking about swans." He'd been thinking a lot of things this afternoon, but there were no swans in all those muddled thoughts. "I sort of brought the Twelve Days of Christmas thing to a close. I mean, how can you give a lord or a lady? And let's not even talk about pipers and drummers."

"I said I had an idea for the rest, but you need to give her a swan yourself. Don't you see? The swan was one of the most important gifts!"

"Nana—"

"Now, listen to me, and I'll tell you why. Back in

Hungary, there was a girl who raised a cygnet after its mother was killed. This swan followed her everywhere. It never left her side if it could help it. When we went to school, it swam in the small pond outside until we were done, then followed us all as we walked home. She loved that swan enough to try to set it free, time and time again, but it loved her enough to always come home."

Nana Vancy paused, then asked, "Do you know why that swan stayed close?"

"It loved her."

She nodded. "But more than that. Swans are monogamous. When they give their hearts, it's forever."

"Then maybe it's good we stopped at swans, because I'm not sure I'm ready to give my heart forever." He sensed that was a lie even as he said the words. There was more truth in his next words. "More than that, I don't know if Eve is."

"You are," Nana said with certainty. "She is. I feel it. And I'm never wrong about these things."

"You were wrong about the curse."

She shook her head. "No, I was right. Only it wasn't really a curse. My words had power after all, and that's why marriages have always meant so much more to my family than their weddings. It will work for you and Eve as well."

"Because words have power?" he repeated.

"Yes. Remember that as I say, *you and Eve are*

meant for each other. You're like swans. You watch. The universe will send you a sign that you're meant to be together."

At that moment, there was the sound of a car pulling into his driveway. Nana beat him to the window and looked out. "Here's your Eve now, and that's my cue to leave. I'll let myself out the back door. But don't forget, watch for the sign, and remember the swans."

Nana Vancy moved very fast for an older woman, because she was gone before Eve even knocked on the door.

TC opened it and immediately took the large box she was holding from her arms. "Come in."

"Tell me you haven't eaten dinner."

"I haven't eaten dinner," he repeated dutifully. The idea of forcing food past the humongous lump in his throat had held no appeal.

Eve smiled as she came into the house and shut the door behind her. "Good. Because I brought it. I hope you don't mind."

At the sight of her smile, the lump in his throat evaporated, and something settled. She was here. No matter what had happened with her ex, she'd come to him. "Of course, I don't mind. But, uh, Eve, this is a very big box for a dinner for two people." The box was huge.

"It's not so much the food as the containers," she said cryptically. "You'll see. Take it into the kitchen, but don't open it."

She took off her coat and followed him into the kitchen. He could hear Bert following her.

He set the box on the counter.

"Sit down, and close your eyes."

He obliged. He could hear the sound of the box opening and things being set on the island's counter.

"Ta-da. Go on, open them."

There on his counter were seven swans—seven swans made out of foil. "I went to this restaurant a few months ago, and they wrapped my leftovers like this. They don't generally even make takeout, but I told them it was a Christmas present of sorts, and they did it for me. Well, for you. Do you like it? I know we said we were done with the Twelve Days, but after six days of gifts from you, I thought it appropriate to give you the swans."

She'd given him swans. He knew he was grinning like a crazy man, but he didn't care. Eve had given him swans. "I love it," he assured her.

She leaned over and kissed his cheek. "Before we eat, I want to say thank you for this afternoon and I'm sorry for ruining your plans."

He reached out and ran a finger over one of the foil swans. Nana had told him there would be a sign, and she was right. This wasn't just one sign but seven. And everyone knew that seven was a lucky number.

He'd always thought of himself as a rational man, but today he believed in signs and lucky numbers. He believed in Nana Vancy's special abilities. "You don't need to apologize for anything, Eve. You're here. That's all that matters."

"Yes, I do. And I need you to understand. I like things nice and orderly. I plan things out. When my ex dumped me, I hadn't seen it coming. I didn't have a clue that he could be the kind of man he showed me he was. I was blindsided, and I felt a bit lost. That's why the job at Salo's was perfect. No unattached men and a lot of files to organize. I was wobbly, but my feet were back under me. I didn't want to date. I just wanted to concentrate on organizing the office and re-organizing me. And then, there you were."

She reached out and touched his cheek softly. "I didn't plan on you either. I didn't count on finding someone who made me wish for mistletoe, someone who made me remember why I clung to believing in Santa Claus. I didn't count on you, you weren't in my plan, and I'm here to tell you, I don't care. I needed to close the books on my ex on my own terms before I could come to you and say that I love you."

"Love." The word that had lingered on his tongue for days rolled out now with no trouble whatsoever. It felt right.

Eve took it as a question, because she immediately assured him, "You don't have to say it back. I know it's too soon, and I didn't plan on saying it either, but it felt right. I don't need anything from you—"

She didn't get any further. TC pulled her into his lap and kissed her. "Nana Vancy was upset that I stopped your Twelve Days of Christmas before the swans. She told me that swans are monogamous. They find that other swan they're meant to be with, and they just stick. Well, Eve, it might be too soon, and I know I don't need to say it, but I love you too. I'm sticking."

He was sticking to Eve like glue. Like a swan.

Later, after they'd spent hours eating and talking about the future—a future together—Eve groaned and leaned against him on the couch. "Do you know what this means?"

"What?" he asked.

"Nana Vancy is going to be more convinced than ever that she's got some kind of weird Hungarian voodoo, and she's going to proceed to fix up the entire city of Erie."

"This sounds so disgustingly unmanly, but I trust you not to ever repeat it to anyone. As far as I'm concerned, Nana Vancy can fix up the whole state of Pennsylvania. Because if she can help other couples feel like we do, then that's not such a bad thing."

"Oh, that was horribly mushy but sweet." She kissed his cheek. "Should we call her and give her the news so she can start planning who to set up next?"

"Later. Right now, there's only you and me. . . ."

"And who needs anything more?"

Bert, as if he knew he'd been excluded, yapped. Eve reached to pat his head. "Sorry, buddy. I know it's a package deal. TC, me, and you."

Seemingly mollified, Bert crawled onto the couch

and flopped down next to Eve, his head resting in her lap.

"You, me, and Bert," she said as she leaned into TC's open arms.

She felt as if she were coming home.

"Home for Christmas," she murmured.

Chapter Fifteen

. . . Maids, Ladies, Lords, Pipers, and Drummers . . .

"You're sure you don't mind spending Christmas Eve with my boss' family?" Eve asked.

TC gave her one of those looks he'd been giving her ever since their swan day. That's how she'd think of it forever . . . the swan day. She took his hand in hers, simply because she couldn't seem to get enough of that. Touching him. Holding him.

"As long as you're there, I don't care," he answered.

"You know, TC, you're eventually going to run out of mushy things to say."

"Not to you."

She opened the Salo Construction office door.

Nana claimed that their Christmas Eve bash was so big, they needed the space. Eve was prepared for more mistletoe and decorations, but she wasn't prepared for the rest. . . .

Nana Vancy, dressed in a Regency-style gown, flanked by two silver-haired women in similar gowns, greeted them. "Eve, TC, these are my dear friends, Isabel and Annabelle."

"They're the Silver Bells," one of the twins—Ricky or Chris, Eve wasn't sure—who was wearing a small drum, called. Matt shushed him, and he said, "What? That's what you guys call 'em."

"Silver Bells. I like it," Annabelle said. "And you do too, Isabel, so don't pretend to be annoyed."

"Aghast," Nana said. "She's not annoyed. She's aghast."

The friends all laughed and then turned their attention back to Eve and TC. Nana asked, "Do you know what this is?"

"No idea," Eve admitted. She looked to TC, who shrugged. "But I can see that TC and I are underdressed."

"See? I told you that they'd be surprised," Nana said with triumph in her voice. "Look at the outfits, you two."

And Eve did. Nana's Bela was wearing a fussy sort of period outfit as well. Dori and Callie, both pregnant to the point of bursting, had on what appeared to be milkmaid outfits. And when Noah saw her looking at him, he grinned and pulled out a small flute and waved it toward her.

Eve started laughing so hard, she could hardly explain to TC when he said, "What?"

"Don't you see? It's the rest of the song. Drummers, pipers, lords, and ladies."

"Maids!" Nana said. "Don't forget the maids!"

"Of course, the maids," TC said as the realization sank in for him as well.

"We wanted you to have the rest of your song," Annabelle said.

"Start the music!" Nana called. And "The Twelve Days of Christmas" started playing. "Now, dance."

"My lady?" TC said.

Eve took his hand and let him lead her to the middle of the floor. The music was too fast for a slow dance and too slow for a fast one, but in the end they simply held each other and moved to their own rhythm.

"You know, I was going to wait for later, but I don't think there will ever be a more perfect moment." He stopped dancing, put a hand into his pocket, and pulled out a box. "I know it's too early, and I know you didn't plan for it, but say you'll marry me, Eve. For a long time I thought I had everything I needed. I never realized that I had this gaping hole in my life—until you came and filled it up."

"You had everything but a Christmas Eve!" Nana crowed.

Eve saw that the entire party had stopped, and, stepping out from behind Nana Vancy, she saw her parents, dressed as a piper and a maid.

Her father nodded, and her mother had tears in her eyes as she smiled.

"Yes, TC. I'll marry you."

He slid the ring onto her finger, then got up, swept her into his arms, and kissed her.

Eve realized she was kissing her fiancé.

The entire room burst into applause.

"Come meet my parents," she said, dragging him to where her parents were standing.

"Mrs. Salo called us and said we would want to be here," her mom said, sweeping her into a hug. "And we were on the next flight."

"Nice to meet you, sir." TC shook her father's hand. "I know we did things out of order, but—"

"I don't want to put a damper on things," Callie said, "but I think it's time for Noah and me to leave and head to the hospital."

"Bill and I were just heading out too," Dori said.

"Well, looks like the Salos' Christmas Eve will be spent in St. Vincent's maternity ward. Come on, everyone."

Eve laughed and traipsed out of the office with everyone else. The entire Salo family. The Silver Bells. Her parents.

And her fiancé.

"You know, Nana Vancy was right," TC said hours later as they sat in a quiet corner of the maternity ward waiting room. "Before you, I had everything . . . everything but a Christmas Eve."

And Eve knew that as long as she had TC, she had everything as well. She kissed him. Kissed the man she loved. The man she'd never planned for and the man she couldn't live without.

"I love you, Mr. Potter."

"And I love you too, soon-to-be Mrs. Allen-Potter. Merry Christmas."

At that moment Noah and Bill hurried into the waiting room. "It a girl! Merry Salo," Noah announced.

"And another girl," Bill said happily. "Christy Hastings."

As the family rushed forward to congratulate the new fathers, Eve turned and kissed her fiancé. "Merry Christmas, TC."

Epilogue

"Auld Lang Syne"

The next December, Eve opened a magazine and read aloud, " 'Every American Man series: I was a Santa for Hire, by TC Potter.' "

> *I imagined writing a quick, quirky column about playing Santa for a week, this Christmas, but instead, I'm writing a column about . . . love.*
>
> *Yes, a year ago, I fell in love wearing a Santa suit.*
>
> *Some of you might remember my inclusion in America's Most Eligible Bachelors a while back. For months I was chased (sometimes literally) and propositioned by marriage-minded women.*
>
> *So I played hermit. I stopped dating. I worked jobs for this column that either offered a good*

disguise (like a mall Santa) or kept me away from females (like my article on living as a monk).

I had a good job, good friends, and good neighbors. I had everything I needed.

And wearing a Santa suit for a week wasn't half bad.

Then I met this amazing woman.

Turns out, in kindergarten I had told her there was no such thing as Santa Claus.

But I later realized I had lied. Because, totally unexpectedly, I fell in love as this woman showed a sick little girl an ugly but lovable necklace and explained that, although there was no magical man who wore a red suit and drove a sleigh pulled by reindeer, there was indeed a real Santa Claus who made a difference in people's lives. It was the heart that loved unconditionally. The soul that gave generously. The smile that made the world a brighter place.

So, while I played Santa, listening to children's Christmas lists, I was trying to decide how to woo this woman, my Christmas Eve.

With a little help from my friends, my wooing took the shape of "The Twelve days of Christmas."

. . . and that is how this American Bachelor, playing Santa Claus, fell in love, wooed his own personal Christmas Eve, and discovered that, yes,

*he'd had everything he needed . . . everything but
his Christmas Eve. And now that he has her, he
has* absolutely *everything.*

*What a beautiful Christmas gift. And for me,
Christmas, when I proposed to her, will always be
our true anniversary.*

Eve set the magazine on the table and kissed her
husband. TC was right. Although they would certainly
celebrate their September wedding anniversary and
delight in memories of their honeymoon in Ireland,
Christmas would always be the time that meant the
most to her . . . the anniversary of when Nana Vancy
Salo matched them up to the tune of "The Twelve
Days of Christmas."

"Happy Anniversary," she said to her husband.

"Happy Anniversary to you too."

"I got you a little something," she said.

"An anniversary gift or a Christmas present?"

"A bit of both. It's actually just the first of your
Christmas presents. There're twelve, in case you're
wondering. One for each day between now and Christmas. But I think you might like this one the best."

TC opened the package, shredding the paper with
true American Man gusto.

He pulled out a baby bib with a partridge in a pear
tree embroidered on it.

"Does this . . . does this mean what I think it means?"

She nodded, tears pooling in her eyes. The doctor had said her hormones might wreak havoc on her emotions, but she didn't think this had anything to do with that, but instead had everything to do with how much she loved her husband.

"You won't even guess the baby's due date. It's June twenty-fourth."

"And that's significant because . . . ?"

"It's half a Christmas Eve."

He laughed, and it was the sweetest sound Eve had ever heard. "I thought if it was a girl we'd name her Noelle, and if it's a boy, Christopher, which is close to *Christmas,* and it's your middle name too—"

The tumbling words were interrupted by her "Fields of Gold" ring tone.

"Go ahead and get it. We have six more months to pick a name."

She answered her phone, "Merry Christmas!"

"Hi, Eve. It's Nana Vancy. I need your help. You see, the Silver Bells and I have found a new case. . . ."